TWICE *in a* LIFETIME

JODIE GRIFFIN

RIPTIDE
PUBLISHING

Riptide Publishing
PO Box 1537
Burnsville, NC 28714
www.riptidepublishing.com

Twice in a Lifetime

Cover art: L.C. Chase, lcchase.com/design.htm
Editors: Sarah Lyons, Carole-ann Galloway
Layout: L.C. Chase, lcchase.com/design.htm

ISBN: 978-1-62649-719-1

First edition
January, 2018

Also available in ebook:
ISBN: 978-1-62649-718-4

TWICE *in a* LIFETIME

JODIE GRIFFIN

RIPTIDE
PUBLISHING

As always, for N. and E. You're my everything.

Table of CONTENTS

Chapter
ONE

With a bounce in my step, I walked into the police station and stopped at the metal detector. I gave a half laugh as the officer at the door told me to put my things on the table. Poor planning on my part. I'd brought two tote bags full of stuff I wanted to put on my desk this first day of my brand-new job. Photos of my girls. A potted plant. A mug that said *World's Okayest Mom*. He looked through the items and lifted the mug out. With a snort, he put it back in, then moved my bags to the far end of the table and waved me forward to the detector.

I stepped through . . . and set the damn buzzer off. I flinched.

He ran the wand over me, up and down my arms and legs, over my back and then my front. When he got to my waist, the thing beeped.

Oh, hell.

"Are you wearing a belt, ma'am?"

If only. "No. But I have a navel piercing with a metal charm on it."

A low female voice came from the line forming behind the metal detector, and an unexpected shiver slid down my spine. "I can verify for you, Ramirez, if you'd like to get all these people moving along."

"Thanks, Lieutenant."

A middle-aged Black woman in a police uniform stepped into view, and my heart sank. My new boss, Lieutenant Eve Poe. *Great. Just great. Way to make an impression.*

"Good morning, Talia. Would you step over here, please?" She led me to a private corner facing away from the people coming into the lobby, which fronted the public entrance to both the police station and the courthouse. "Standard procedure."

I must've turned purple, but after I looked over my shoulder to make sure no one was staring, I lifted the edge of my blouse and nudged down the waist of my trousers. "I meant to take it out before I came to work, but I forgot."

My stomach fluttered when her deep-brown eyes lingered maybe a fraction of a second too long before she nodded. "Good enough. Usually piercings don't set off the detectors. Not sure why this one did."

"My lucky day?" I quipped, trying to cover my embarrassment—and my unsettled libido. I'd only met her twice before this, once during a Citizen's Police Academy class I'd taken when my daughters were little, and once a few weeks ago during my interview for this community liaison job. Both times, I'd had the same instant reaction to the woman in front of me. A visceral attraction, simmering under the surface, an awareness I'd only ever had with one other person in my life. My late husband, Seth.

She grinned then, and it changed her angular brown face from average to heart-stoppingly gorgeous in a single beat. This was the smile I remembered from that long-ago class, one that had zinged me when I'd had no business being zinged. And it was a grin that had recently fueled some intense fantasies while I'd waited for my paperwork and background checks for this job to clear.

Focus, Talia.

She led me back to the officer manning the metal detector. "Talia Wasserman, this is Officer First Class Juan Ramirez. Juan, Talia's the new civilian community liaison working in my office. She'll get her credentials today."

"Yes, ma'am."

Lieutenant Poe—*Eve*, I reminded myself—led us down the hallway to a small office at the end of the floor. She unlocked the door, and nudged it open with her hip. "I'm usually here earlier than this, but I had a personal issue to deal with. And I left my access pass at home, which is why I had to come in the public entrance." She grimaced as though she'd tasted something sour, then shook her head and pointed to the desk that faced hers. "Anyway, make yourself at home. Supply cabinet is in the next office. I need about fifteen minutes to get my system up and running, and then we can get your laptop from IT and pick up your building ID. Once you have that, you can park out back with the rest of the employees and avoid the whole metal-detector thing."

"Sounds good." I moved around my new-to-me but probably forty-year-old desk and dropped into the chair, which creaked. Obviously the police department didn't spend much money on office furniture. I had plenty of my own padding on my ass, but I was going to need a cushion or I'd wreck my back inside of a week. I pulled out my phone and jotted a reminder—because *what brain?*—and noticed I'd gotten two texts during my fifteen-minute commute this morning, one from each of my girls.

I glanced at my new boss before taking a minute to open the texts. I didn't want it to look like I was goofing off first day on the job, but they were my babies.

I read Rissa's text first. *Have a good first day. Keep your eyes open for hot cops to date. For me, not for you. Okay, for you too. Love you, Mom.*

My eyes flew to Eve. Did she count as hot? Well, for a woman who was probably close to my own fifty-two and was in incredible physical condition, yeah. She did. My stomach fluttered again, and I turned my attention back to my phone. *Thanks, sweetie. Love you too. I'll call you tonight.*

Lila's text was next. At her prodding this morning, I'd sent her a picture of what I was wearing to the office. **whistles* You're one hot mama, Mama.* I smiled and kept reading. *You've got this. Love ya!*

I texted her back. *LOL! Love you too. You still coming over for dinner?*

I was so lucky. My girls were one hundred percent awesome, and I was proud of the young women they'd become. Lila had decided college wasn't for her and had instead gone to trade school to become an electrician, and Rissa was away at her second year of college studying engineering. There were times when they'd been teens that I'd understood why some species ate their young, but once they'd passed into adulthood, things had evened back out.

I set my phone down and looked up to see Eve watching me.

"Everything okay?"

"Texts from my daughters." I smiled, then pulled out my favorite-ever mug and the plant Lila had given me from a cutting she'd made me from the one I'd given her for her apartment. Full circle, which amused me. "First-day-on-the-job good-luck wishes."

"How old are they?" She leaned forward, tapped a few keys, and frowned, tapping a few more.

"Lila's almost twenty-four and Rissa is twenty."

"It's nice they keep in touch." She sounded almost wistful. "My son is twenty-five. He's a Marine deployed to Iraq, so I don't get to talk to him too often."

"Oh, that's hard." My heart clenched. I couldn't imagine fearing for my girls day in and day out. Not that I didn't worry about them. I absolutely did. But not *they're in a war zone* worry. That had to be a special hell for a parent.

It took a moment for her words to click in another way, and when they did, my heart stuttered. She was married? I glanced at her hands. No rings. I wanted to smack myself, though. It didn't matter, because there were a few teeny tiny items I needed to remember.

First, she was my boss.

Second, I had no idea if she was interested in women.

And third, even if she was, *I* had exactly zero experience in being with another woman. Fantasized about it, felt the attraction and the sexual desire, but had never put any of that to the test.

I berated myself for thinking of this now. *First day on a new job, remember?*

I locked my libido away and spent the next fifteen minutes grabbing supplies from the cabinet—notepads, sticky notes, pens, a ruler—and organizing things on my desk. By the time I was done, so was Eve.

"Ready for a full tour?"

"I'd love one, thanks. And while I hate to sound like a typical addict, is there coffee?"

"There is, in the squad room and also in the lunch room. Sorry I didn't think about it. I'm not a coffee drinker. I prefer tea."

I eyed her suspiciously. "Really? I didn't know people like you actually existed."

She let out a full-bodied laugh that blasted my good intentions all to hell. "A snarky sense of humor. We're going to get along just fine, Talia."

As we left our office, she brushed against me. I swear I'm not a sex-crazed maniac, but the electric jolt I got from her innocent touch made me reconsider my opinion of myself. I cleared my throat and tried hard not to notice the amazing way her ass filled out the khaki uniform pants she wore.

We spent much of the morning hunched over Eve's desk as she showed me the calendar she kept for community events. My mind was boggled by the sheer number of requests that came through the office, and I told her so.

"I can't believe you've been managing this by yourself for so long," I added.

She sighed, leaning back in her chair. "It hasn't been all that long, though it feels like it. Your predecessor was the organizational genius on this team. When her husband retired, they decided to move to Florida. Can't blame her, but she left a giant hole. I'm barely holding it together." She sat back up, flashed teeth. "Not that I want to scare you away from the job or anything."

I couldn't help but laugh. "Oh, it takes a lot to scare me off." The minute the words left my mouth, I mentally cringed. *Stop it, Talia.*

"Duly noted." She grinned, then glanced at the clock. "Time for lunch."

I startled. "Already? Wow, the morning went fast. An hour, right?"

She nodded. "How does Thai sound to you?"

I blinked. I'd brought yogurt and a piece of fruit, which would take me just a few minutes to eat. "I figured I'd eat at my desk and then go for a walk to get some fresh air and exercise."

"I try to take my new people out for lunch their first day. It's a chance to get to know each other a little better, away from the office." She tilted her head, and gave me a puzzled look when I didn't answer right away. "Unless you'd rather not?"

"No, I'd love to. Thank you." When her confusion slid into a slow grin, I got yet another zing, this time low in my belly. Oh, hell, I was in so much trouble.

Do not, under any circumstances, flirt with your new boss, Talia. Do. Not.

We walked to the restaurant, which was only about two blocks away. People clearly knew Eve, liked her, and it was patently obvious how important community relations were to her. She smiled and chatted with shopkeepers and passersby and, at one point, crouched to show her badge to a fascinated preschooler. It took us a full fifteen minutes to get to the Thai place, but if we were late getting back, who would complain? She was the boss. Mine, anyway.

They took us to a table immediately, even though there were others waiting. I flicked a glance at the line, where several grumpy businessmen stood, frowning. She followed my gaze and grinned. "I promise we're not getting special privileges. I called Friday and reserved a table. Dudes should've tried that and not assumed they'd get a seat right away, at noon on a workday."

I agreed. We sat, and I picked up the menu, scanning the whole thing. I didn't know too much about Thai food, but every single description sounded good. "Do you recommend anything special here?"

"It's *all* good. Which is why I'm going to get the buffet." She glanced down at her flat stomach and sighed. "Of course, at my age, that'll require extra sit-ups tonight. My metabolism went haywire when I hit forty-five."

I choked on a laugh. Nothing but the truth there. Once I hit my late forties, everything I looked at or smelled landed on my hips. Eve and I were close to the same height, but I probably had fifty pounds on her. I waved my hand in the general direction of my thicker-than-in-my-twenties waist. "You seem to be handling it much better than I am."

"Have to, for the job. It's easier because I'm always on the move. I spend half my workday out and about." She paused, gave her head a little shake as though she'd changed her mind about what she was going to say. Then she spoke anyway, the words coming as a fast barrage. "If you're interested, I run every morning before work and shower at the station. You can join me if you'd like." She swore softly and pushed up from the table. "That . . . did not come out right. I just meant that if you're interested in getting some exercise with me, I'm game." Air hissed out from between her lips as she muttered something indecipherable under her breath.

Oh, good lord. Exercise? Shower? Now my mind was going places it really shouldn't be going because hello, my *boss* for a job I both wanted and needed. I kept my tone light and shoved the inappropriate thoughts away. "I may take you up on that. I used to run, and I always felt better afterward."

I followed her to the buffet. Since I didn't know what anything was, she pointed out the different dishes to me. People gave her space—you know, woman with a badge and a gun—but crowded me as I tried to decide what to choose. The person behind me bumped into me twice, and then I felt a hand fondle my ass. I turned and sent him a withering glare. He was one of the men who'd been waiting for a table, and he now held an empty carryout box. He was close to my age, maybe mid-fifties, and I'd met so many men like him after Seth died.

Instead of looking ashamed, he gave me what he likely thought was a sexy grin, but it was wolfish and not at all welcome. If he assumed I was the kind of woman who'd take it quietly, or who'd fall at his feet for even being noticed at my age, he was sadly mistaken.

"If you touch my ass again, I'm going to knee you in the balls. I don't care who you are, and I don't care who sees it. Are we clear?"

Eve turned sharply at that and delivered a frosty, one hundred percent cop stare in his direction.

He almost tripped over himself apologizing. "It was an accident. My apologies, ma'am." He didn't look my way again as he filled his carryout box, and kept a good foot between us.

Eve and I went back to our table, where the waiter had filled our water glasses, and sat.

"Jesus, it's no wonder I only date women." Eve picked up her fork, stabbed at her food. "You okay? You handled that like a pro."

I couldn't help but laugh, even as my heart stuttered at her revelation about her sexuality. "I'm a little shaken, but it doesn't trigger anything for me except contempt, if that's what you mean. I've never been . . . I'm one of the lucky ones."

"You are." Her eyes clouded over, then cleared. "That's one of the reasons I like being a cop and working in this department. Women should be able to feel safe wherever they are. They sure as hell shouldn't get their asses grabbed—or worse—in a restaurant, or at school, or walking down the street. And kids—both girls *and* boys—need to learn that early on, so Community Relations is incredibly important."

I started eating. The food was decadently good, and I let out a noise that was almost embarrassing. "Exactly. I worry about my girls more than I worry about myself, honestly. But since my husband died, you'd be surprised at how many men think I should be grateful for their attention, especially at my age." I paused, fork to my mouth. "Or maybe you wouldn't."

A tiny smile quirked her full, lush lips. "You're right, I wouldn't." Her smile faded. "I know this is going to sound weird, but we've met before, haven't we? I feel like we have, only I'm drawing a blank at *where*."

So much for my zing moment being something we'd shared. I'd put the Citizen's Police Academy training on my application, but we hadn't discussed it in detail during my interview. "We have. It's been a while, though. I'm surprised you remember. I'm sure you meet a lot of people."

Her grin flashed again, and damn it, it still affected me. "I do. Are you going to tell me when and where? Or do I have to guess?"

"I think you should guess."

This time she laughed outright. "We really are going to get along great. Clue me in, Talia."

I grinned back. "About fifteen years ago. You helped at the practical exercise day for the Citizen's Police Academy class I took. You showed me how to fire a gun during our target practice. I kept missing the target completely and everyone in my group was laughing at me for being such a mess, so you got behind me and helped steady my stance."

I had never forgotten the feel of her body against mine, the heat of her chest against my back, even though we'd both been wearing body armor that day. Her hands had been warm and capable and strong, and her minty breath had fanned across my cheek. I'd been incredibly, blissfully married to Seth, but she'd made me think things I'd had no business thinking as a married woman. She'd made me wonder, for the first time in a very long time, *What if?*

Her eyes widened, and she set down her fork and took a long swallow of her water. "Christ. I . . . Yeah. I remember now." She blinked, picked up her fork again, and pointed it at me. "You *did* suck at that."

I snorted. "Which is why you're the cop, and I'm the civilian."

"Good point."

Between bites of food, we got to know each other. I told her becoming a widow at forty-eight had knocked me for a loop, and how excited I was about this job and the new chapter in my life now that my girls were out and on their own, though I was looking forward to having them both home for the holidays. She told me how she'd started out as a beat cop right out of college, how she worried about her only child being deployed in a war zone, and how she couldn't wait to see him when he came home on leave at Thanksgiving. Conversation flowed as though we'd known each other for years, and the half hour passed quickly. Eve paid the tab, and we left, making our way back to the police station. When we got there, I took off my jacket and sat, but Eve stayed on her feet.

"I hate to do this to you on your first day, but I've got an unavoidable meeting from two until five. Can you answer the phones and take notes on what people are looking for? I'll deal with it when I get back. I'd rather have them speak to someone than make them leave a voicemail. More personal, less bureaucratic. And check group email too. Respond if you can, and if you can't, forward them to me."

"Answer phones? Send email? No problem." I smiled at her. "You're the boss, so you tell me what to do, and I do it, whatever it is."

It wasn't until I caught her raised brow that I realized what I'd said, and heat rushed into my cheeks. But she let it slide, maybe because of her own unintended innuendo earlier. "Thanks, Talia. Don't wait for me to get back, because it's likely we'll go past five."

I nodded. "I'll see you tomorrow. Thanks for lunch."

She picked up a thick folder from her desk and headed toward the door, then glanced back over her shoulder at me. "I'm glad to have you on board."

Chapter
TWO

When I walked in the house after work, I found Lila sitting at the kitchen table, twisting paper napkins into confetti.

My motherly instincts went on red alert. "You're here early, honey. Is everything okay?"

She wrinkled her nose—the one she'd gotten from Seth and shared with her sister and her cousins due to some seriously strong family genes—and stilled her hands. "Not really, no. I mean, nothing I haven't heard a thousand times before, y'know? But I'm getting sick of it."

"Let me guess. A customer wouldn't let you touch his stuff because you're a woman." Lila had worked for Seth's brother for almost three years now and loved being part of a family business with her cousins—and breaking down stereotypes of what women could do—but she rarely went a week without a homeowner questioning her abilities.

She wadded the shredded napkins into a ball. "Yep. And Uncle Noah had my back like he always does, but I hate that he has to do it. How long do I have to keep proving myself?" Before I could answer, she waved it away. "I know, I know. And I knew what I was getting into, but I like this work. I'm good at it too." Her pretty blue eyes flashed and her chin went up. "I'm better at it than Jacob is. Even he says so."

Jacob was her cousin, Noah's son. He'd never shown interest in being an electrician, but he'd once told her that, as the oldest, he'd felt like he had to join the family business. He'd been a straight-A student who had an affinity for numbers and was better suited to run the business, not do the field work. The sooner Noah pulled his head out of his ass, the better off they'd all be. I nodded, then kept prodding. "So, what else is bugging you?"

More napkin shredding.

"I went to surprise Ryan today because the job site was close to his office, and he always goes out for lunch at noon. I pulled up just in time to . . ." She hunched her shoulders and her eyes filled. "To see him in a lip-lock with some other woman."

If Ryan had been standing here with us, I would've given him hell for breaking my girl's heart. "Oh, honey. I'm sorry." I drew her to her feet and into a hug. "Did he see you?"

She squeezed me once, really hard, then let go and paced the room. Of my daughters, Lila was the one who was always on the move. "He did. He seemed surprised I was upset. I don't even know what the hell he was thinking." She snorted. "Or maybe I do. She was gorgeous, tall, and model-thin with tiny but perky boobs. Pretty much everything I'm not."

My eldest child was barely five two and what Seth's mother called *zaftig*. Her curves had curves, but she was beautiful—inside and out— and damn Ryan for making her feel bad about herself. "Perky boobs are overrated. They'll sag eventually."

Lila laughed, as I'd hoped, but she was obviously hurt by his infidelity. Who wouldn't be? They'd only been dating a few months, but I knew she'd thought maybe he would be *the one*. "Anyway, I told him to come get his stuff this weekend. I already texted Yas and Tee to come over at the same time so I don't do anything stupid like take him back."

I hid a grin. The three were best friends and had been since middle school. In their teens, they'd protected each other from cruel classmates who'd taunted them for their *otherness*—Jewish girl, Muslim girl, gay Black girl. Many friends had come and gone, but Lila, Yasmin, and Tamara had stayed close, and I was grateful. "Good. But don't let Yasmin near him. Didn't she just get her third-degree black belt?"

"Yep." She rubbed her eyes and squared her shoulders. "So, enough about that. Tell me about your new job. How's your boss?"

I hugged her again, then nudged her to the fridge. "The job is good. Get some veggies out, would you? I'm making stir-fry with shrimp I picked up tonight."

She whirled toward me and gaped. "Shrimp? Mom, no."

I grinned. "Gotcha. I got chicken." Seth and I had decided to raise our kids as practicing Jews, and that had included keeping a kosher house. He'd been more diligent about it than I was—he'd been raised that way, and I hadn't—but I still tried my best, especially around the girls.

"That was just mean."

I opened a cupboard and pulled out my wok. "I know."

Lila giggled, and the sound warmed me. "Does your boss know you're a smart-ass?"

I laughed. "Oh, she knows. I think she's the same way, so it should be a fun place to work."

Lila plopped half the contents of the vegetable bin on the counter. "Any hot cops out there? I mean, now that I'm single again?"

The only one I noticed was her. I wasn't ready to say that to my kid, so I reached out and tugged her hair. "I'll keep my eyes open. But I have to warn you, your sister asked first."

"Hah. I talked to Rissa yesterday. Sounds like she's digging her classes this semester. I was worried. She seemed stressed out about going back to school over the summer."

Yeah, I'd been worried too. My youngest child was an overthinker, and she'd convinced herself she should stay home and take classes locally. I knew, though, that she'd always wanted to go to Seth's alma mater, and when she'd gotten in, it had been a Really. Big. Deal. Once I got her to understand we wanted that for her too—both Lila and I—she'd gone back. And she was thriving. "That's what she told me, especially the mechanical engineering one. And I'm glad you two talk."

"Well, duh." She lined all the veggies up in size order from baby carrots to zucchini, which amused me to no end. "We're plotting against you."

I snort-laughed. "Lovely."

I studied my daughter's too-pale face as she concentrated on chopping the vegetables, maybe with a little more force than was needed, but who was I to stop her from venting her frustrations? She still looked upset, but less so by the time she was done, and I hoped talking about normal things was helping ease the pain of betrayal. I still wanted to hurt Ryan, but if my daughter could deal, so could I.

"Tell me about work."

So I did exactly that as I cooked, including the fact that I'd met Eve before, but excluding the fact that I'd been attracted to her. Though same-sex relationships weren't any different than hetero relationships to my girls—we knew a lot of people on the LGBTQ rainbow—I wasn't sure how they would deal with me being attracted to someone *not* their father, even after four years.

By the time I was finished talking, dinner was ready. After I said the blessing, we ate.

Lila took a bite of broccoli. "It sounds like a lot of fun. Will you get grief about not working on Shabbat?"

"I don't think so. There may be weekend events, but right now it looks like I'll take the ones on Sundays. But if I have to, I have to. I'm sure others have to work on days they'd normally be in church or have other obligations."

"True." She swiped a piece of chicken around her barely touched plate. "Mom? Why do they do shit like that?"

I knew what she meant immediately. "I don't know why some do, but they don't all. Dad didn't. And the good ones will break up with you before they move on. Still painful, but at least they're not being jerks about it." I reached out and squeezed her hand. "But if he's the cheating kind, better you know now than later."

"Yeah." She tore apart a dinner roll, sighed, then set it down. "Pretty sure I'm done with guys for a while. First Ben. Then Ryan."

Ben was a kid she'd known since preschool at the synagogue, and they'd dated on and off through high school. They'd been prom dates, but I'd never seen them really click. "Oh, honey. The right guy is out there for you, somewhere, and there's no hurry. I want you to have fun before you settle down, anyway. Travel, do what you want to do before the responsibility of kids and mortgages. Speaking of which, where are you and Tee and Yas going for vacation this year?"

She brightened slightly. "One of the Comic-Cons. We're still trying to figure out which. Maybe San Diego. There's a lot to do there outside the con too."

I had to laugh. These girls—women, yes, but always girls to me since I'd known them forever—had been crazy over comic books and action movies based off of them for as long as I could remember. "Sounds like a great idea."

Not long after we finished, she headed home because her work day started early. Mine would too, and I found myself looking forward to it, to being at work.

To seeing Eve.

While I loaded the dishwasher, I gave myself a stern talking-to about keeping things with Eve purely professional. When I was done with both the dishes and the lecture, I locked up and went upstairs. I'd taken the night off from the class that I taught at the synagogue, because I'd figured I'd be exhausted after my first day. It had been a good decision.

I stepped into my bedroom. This past spring, I'd decided it was time for me to move on, but I'd cried ugly tears as I'd covered over the blue walls Seth and I had painted together ten years earlier. The weekend we'd done it, the girls had been away on some scout trip, and we'd had the house to ourselves. We'd gotten so much paint on us that we'd shucked our clothes and had wound up making love on the drop cloth–covered carpet. I'd had a blue handprint on my ass that had lasted for weeks.

Painting the room had been painful but cathartic. The walls were now a light lavender, a color Seth had hated but I loved. I wouldn't say the room was frilly, but I'd definitely added more feminine touches to it. I'd treated myself to new furniture too, moving our old things to the room that had been the girls' playroom. It was a big space, nice for my parents to stay in when they came north from Florida to visit.

As always, when I dropped my jewelry onto the dresser, I touched Seth's picture. I missed him every damn day, and probably always would, even if I found someone else. Twenty-three years was a lot of time together, and sometimes it was still hard to believe he was gone. He'd been my other half, and I'd been devastated by his death. But he *was* gone, and I wasn't. I didn't think he'd begrudge me finding someone to fill my days and nights, someone to share my thoughts and hopes and dreams with.

After a quick call with Rissa, who asked me if we could talk another night since she was studying for an exam, I got ready for bed, grabbed my Kindle, and settled in with my favorite mystery writer.

I woke just as the alarm went off, which was nothing short of a miracle. Usually it took me several smacks of the Snooze button to get my ass out of bed. Which explained why I had said ass, probably. When the girls had been little, I'd risen early and run with two of the other moms on the block while our husbands had gotten the kids ready for school, but it had been years since I'd run. Was I really considering starting again, running with Eve before work?

Maybe, but not today. I'd have to set my alarm even earlier than this, and I had to build up to that.

Since I had my credentials and could use the employee door now, I left my belly button ring in. Getting it had been one of those spur-of-the-moment things I'd done after Seth died, egged on by my girls after I'd admitted that I thought they were cool. It had hurt like a son of a bitch and taken forever to heal, but I loved it.

I showered, then dressed for work—khakis and scoop-neck thin sweater—and headed down to the kitchen. It only took me fifteen minutes to get to the police station, so I drank a cup of coffee before pouring myself a second in a travel mug.

When I got to the office, it was still early. I didn't start until eight, and it wasn't quite seven thirty. I noticed Eve's computer was already on, and my pulse tripped.

We talked about this, remember? Boss. Off-limits.

I got my session started, then checked the office email account. It had been empty when I'd left at five. And now there were twenty messages. Goodness.

I opened up each and, if I could, provided the information Eve had shown me yesterday. By the time I'd gone through all of them, there were only five that would take more knowledge than I'd learned in my first day at work.

"You're here early."

I jumped, my heart thudding. "I . . . Yeah." That was all I could manage to spit out, because she'd obviously just come in from a run. Her face glistened with sweat, and the thin jacket she wore over running tights and a sports bra did nothing to hide the fact that it was, indeed, colder outside than it looked. I dragged my gaze up her lean body and flushed as amusement flashed in her bright eyes. I cleared my throat and forced myself to focus. "I thought I'd get started on the overnight requests so we had time for you to show me some other things I could maybe take off your plate."

Her amusement turned to speculation, and then approval. "You're my kind of people, Talia Wasserman. Thank you. Give me a few minutes to clean up, and we can get started."

True to her word, she was back in fifteen minutes, in uniform, her hair smoothed into a neat twist, a light gloss on her lips. She held a steaming mug of tea in her hand.

As she pulled her chair up and sat, I smelled apples and cinnamon. I didn't know if it was her tea or whatever she'd used in the shower but—*stop thinking about it, Talia.*

"I wasn't sure what to do with these." I pointedly ignored my libido and opened up the first email. "This one isn't a Community Relations request. It sounds like they have a problem with an investigation."

"Forward it to me, and I'll look up the case to see who's handling it. If you get these, send them to me. I can't get you access to that system since that's active casework and not public information."

"No problem. I just needed to know how to handle it." I pulled up the next one. "This one was a little . . ." I paused, considered my words. "Off, maybe? I couldn't put my finger on it. Not a threat, exactly. But weird phrasing. *Lady cops should be careful out there.*"

She leaned forward, read it, and then frowned. "Good intuition. We've gotten a couple like this one, and from the same IP address. One of them specifically mentioned the promenade along the creek where the upcoming street festival is being held. Delia Butler is the detective handling the investigation. Forward anything like them to her and copy me. The festival is only a few weeks away. We'll have a large presence there, but she and I are trying to get to the bottom of it before then. Any odd phone calls or emails or regular mail that implies a threat or a disturbance for that event, let me and Delia know ASAP. Even if there's no direct threat but it feels off to you."

"Understood."

She flashed the briefest of smiles. "Nature of the beast, unfortunately. You'll get used to it. What's next?"

Goodness, I hope so. I forwarded the message as directed, then opened the next one. "College student asking if she can interview you for a term paper she's doing on women in law enforcement."

Eve raised a brow. "And you needed to ask me about this one personally, why?"

I grinned. "Because I wanted to see your reaction?"

She laughed. "Fair enough. Yes. Find a spot on my calendar and schedule her in. I don't love these, but I'll do them. Especially for other women. What else?"

I pulled up the next email. "This one they're looking for a school visit. Pretty standard and we went over how to schedule those, but I had an idea for it."

She leaned close and read the email, her shoulder brushing mine. I sucked in a breath, and when she leaned back, I finally breathed again.

"Okay, so what's your suggestion?"

"Since this is a special education preschool, I thought maybe bringing a police dog might break the ice. Most kids love dogs, and it might strengthen the lesson you give. I know we'd have to check with the school about allergies or any other issues first, but . . ."

A broad smile landed on her face. "I'd say you're a great fit for this job. It's an excellent idea. Go ahead and set it up. Jake Watanabe is one of our K-9 handlers, and he's training a new puppy. That might be fun for them."

I nodded, then opened the last email I'd wanted to ask her about. But before we could go over it, there was a loud commotion in the hallway, with shouting and sounds of a scuffle.

Eve surged to her feet, pointing at me even as she raced for the door. "Stay in here. You do not leave this room. Got it?"

I swallowed. "I . . . Yes."

She was only gone a few minutes—a few really long minutes— and when she came back, she was shaking her head, disgust etched on her face.

"Is everything okay?"

"Oh, fine, except two recruits from this year's academy class are about to get their asses chewed out for brawling in the hallway. What the hell were they thinking, anyway?" She didn't let me answer, just continued. "They weren't. They were too busy comparing test scores— and dick sizes."

I couldn't help myself, and a snort escaped.

The corner of her mouth turned up. "Were we ever that young? Hard to remember."

"We must've been. But the fighting thing—I never got that. My late husband, Seth, and his brother used to get into it all the time. We were, what? Twenty-three, twenty-four? Men—especially young ones—are a mystery to me. I only have girls. And right now, I'm thinking all guys that age are pains in the ass." After the words were out of my mouth, I remembered Eve had a son who was that age, and tried to clarify. "My daughter caught her boyfriend cheating on her yesterday."

Eve winced. "That's bad. But really, they're not all that way. Derrick has his head on pretty straight for a twenty-five-year-old man. At least, I hope he does. Hard to tell from half a world away."

Her eyes grew troubled, and I cursed my unthinking words. "I'm sorry. I shouldn't have said that."

She blinked. "What? No, it wasn't that. I was just thinking about his call yesterday. It's why I was late getting here, why I left my access pass at home. He told me he had something to tell me, but we got cut off. I haven't been able to get in touch with him since. Not unusual to have unreliable phone service, but I have no idea what he was going to tell me." A half smile, half grimace twisted her lips even as her eyes grew shadowed. "You're a parent. I'm sure you can imagine the things going through my head."

"Yeah. I can." My heart clenched in sympathy. I held up my coffee cup. "I'm going to get a refill. Can I get you anything?"

She peered into her empty mug. "You don't mind? It's definitely not part of the job."

"I don't mind," I said, smiling.

"Just some hot water, then. Thank you." Her computer *ding*ed, and her eyes drifted to her screen. The minute she started reading she looked completely absorbed, so I picked up her mug and mine and went down to the break room.

There was a redheaded woman at the counter, waiting for the pot of coffee to finish. She was dressed in street clothes with a badge clipped to her waist. As I came in, she smiled and her sharp eyes flicked to the ID around my neck.

"Oh, hey. You're Eve's new assistant." She held out her hand. "I'm Delia Butler."

I shook her hand. "Talia Wasserman. Nice to meet you. I just sent you an email."

She grimaced. "I got it, thanks. This makes three. Did Eve tell you if you get anything else like that—email, post office mail, phone call—to let us know?"

"She did." I paused, not sure if I was stepping somewhere I shouldn't, considering I wasn't a cop. "Is this something she needs to worry about? Even to me, it sounded creepy."

"Not sure yet. Some people are looking for attention. Others have darker things in mind. I'm investigating." She frowned. "And since I'm on limited duty, it gets my full attention." I must've seemed confused, because she smiled wryly and motioned to her waist. "Pregnant. Just starting my second trimester."

I smiled. "Congratulations. Is this your first?"

She fiddled with a shamrock charm on a chain around her neck. "Yes. And considering my husband's reaction to the first trimester, he or she might be an only child. You have kids?"

"I do. Two girls, one in college, one working. And I know what you mean. When I was pregnant with Lila, my first, I had morning sickness all day long. My late husband got a little overbearing and kept telling me what I could and couldn't do."

"Sounds like Colin." Delia grinned and rolled her eyes, but then her smile faded. "Anyway, keep me posted if anything else comes across your desk. As a female cop, this makes me twitchy. And as a cop, period, I hate having this hanging over our heads this close to the festival, when the streets will be jam-packed with people."

I'd been to it before, and I knew she spoke the truth. My stomach knotted, and I swallowed over the lump sitting in my throat. "I will."

Chapter
THREE

Work settled into a comfortable routine. I got in around seven thirty every day, even though I didn't get paid for that extra half hour. I liked the quiet mornings where I could slice and dice the request mailbox into things I could handle and things that needed Eve's attention. It felt good to be able to take some of the stress off her, and I tried not to think about why I felt that way.

The more I got to know her, the more I liked her. She was book-smart and life-smart and really cared about the community she served. She stayed patient with me and gave freely of her time, even when it might be faster to just do something herself. And she was wickedly funny, with a dry humor I would bet many people didn't understand. My physical attraction to her was still there too, and it continued to grow.

We spent a few hours a week out and about at different events. The college student's interview had been eye-opening for me, and I'd learned quite a bit about my boss and what it had taken for her to get where she was. The preschool visit had been a big hit with the kids, and the K-9 puppy had stolen the show.

The six weeks I'd been there had flown, and I was having the time of my life.

Today was Friday, the last day before my first weekend event with the department. Sunday was the street festival that had been taking up most of our planning time, where several blocks in the downtown area would be roped off. There would be food and art and activities for kids to do.

We'd received one more email that mentioned the festival, and another that just said female cops needed to be careful. No outward threats, but a warning that something might happen.

I'd learned there would be a large officer presence at the festival, both as part of the event and policing it. Eve and Delia had met several times about the issue, and I knew they'd also met with the team who'd be responsible for public safety.

Eve's confidence should've calmed me, but I was still uneasy. Maybe because it was my first event. Or maybe it was because, as a female cop, Eve could be a target.

As I printed fliers we'd be handing out, I glanced at Eve's empty desk, then back at the clock. It was eight thirty and I hadn't heard from her or seen her. I'd grown used to finding her things here when I arrived in the morning. I decided everyone had the right to sleep late some days, and besides, she was the boss. I finished with the fliers and began to gather all the promotional items we'd need for Sunday. If she wasn't here by ten, I'd start to worry.

A few minutes before ten, she came in. Her posture was rigid, and she all but slammed her stuff down on her desk. Her voice came out in a low growl, a tone I'd never heard from her before. "What'd I miss?"

I winced. "Ah, nothing much? I printed everything off for Sunday. You okay?"

She sucked in a long breath and blew it out slowly. "No, but I will be. It's nothing work related, but it put me in a foul mood. I don't mean to take it out on you."

"I raised teenagers. This is nothing." I said them matter-of-factly, but my words seemed to put her on edge. "Eve?"

"That damn fool son of mine got himself engaged to a girl I've never even met." She swore, low and profane. "She's a civilian reporter he kept talking about, but engaged? Good lord." I started to speak, but she waved me off with a deep sigh. "I can't think about it right now. We've got things to do before the festival."

She dropped into her chair with complete lack of her usual grace, then grimaced at her empty mug.

Well, I could fix this, at least. "Read your mail. Take a few deep breaths. I'll go get your tea." She opened her mouth as if to protest, but I smiled gently. "Read. Breathe. When you think you're settled, breathe some more."

She sighed, then rolled her shoulders. "Thanks, Talia. Really."

"Any time."

Eve was laser-focused for the rest of the day. She brought me out to the large mobile command center we'd use to do child fingerprinting and showed me how to do what I'd need to do. We sat side by side at the small table, so close our knees pressed together. Her skin felt warm and smooth as she picked up my hand to ink my fingers, and I trembled at the contact. *Get a grip, Talia.*

Her brown eyes flicked to mine, and maybe it was my imagination, but I swore her voice deepened ever so slightly.

"Kids will wiggle a lot, so you have to talk to them the whole time you're taking their prints. Here's how you do the ink," she said, rolling my thumb across the pad. "And here's how you get it on the paper." She did another finger, and then handed me a cloth to wipe the ink off. "Now, you do me."

There was dead silence for a moment, but I couldn't help myself. I tried, really I did, but I let out a snort-laugh, covering my mouth as I glanced over at Eve's face. "I'm sorry. I know. Twelve-year-old boy. I . . ." I dissolved into wholly inappropriate laughter.

Eve just shook her head, but the amusement in her eyes was obvious. "Talia, Talia. What am I going to do with you?"

I laughed again as I twisted her words into dirty ones, but it was more of a giggle-snort. We'd hit it off from the very first and, after working closely with her for the past six weeks, I felt comfortable teasing her. Boss or not. "Oh, come on. You can't tell me you weren't thinking the same thing."

An unrestrained grin flashed on her face. "That predictable, huh?"

"Let's just say I appreciate your sense of humor because it is very, very similar to mine." I picked up her hand, trying to stifle my body's response to her as I inked her thumb and rolled it on the paper.

Once again, her voice had a slightly husky edge to it. "A little smudged, but not bad. Do all ten, and if the fingerprint tech can read it, we'll consider this a success and you can help with them at the festival. It's probably the busiest part of our area, and we can use all the help we can get."

When we finished up with that, we stocked all the things we were bringing for the kids—sticker badges, coloring books—and brochures for their parents with information on internet safety, drug awareness, and bike clinics.

To my dismay, she also showed me how to sound the alarm if there was an issue, how to tune into the radio frequency everyone would be using—and how to respond if necessary. She leaned against the counter, arms crossed, and watched me as I tried to absorb everything I might need to know if things went all to hell.

"Breathe, Talia." I swiveled my head toward her, thinking she was teasing me by using words I'd used earlier, but she wasn't smiling. "This festival and our mystery emailer do create a potentially serious situation. I'm not going to lie to you about that. The day should be fun for everyone, but we will have to keep our eyes open. This afternoon, we'll do a final run-through of what we know about him or her in the command room with the entire team of people working on Sunday, along with contingency plans. I'd like you to come with me."

I swallowed hard, but nodded. I stayed quiet as we went back inside, and after spending almost all day together for six weeks, Eve understood me enough to realize I needed a few minutes to process what she'd told me. She pointed me toward the lab and, while she went back to our office, I gave the tech the samples I'd made and waited to see if I'd passed or failed Fingerprinting 101.

I passed.

When I got back to our office, Eve was on the phone, her brow furrowed as she listened to whoever was on the other end. Her eyes were closed, and she was rubbing a thumb against her temple.

Then, as though a switch had been flipped, her hand dropped and her eyes popped open. "Excuse me?" She caught me hovering at the threshold and waved me in. "Isaiah Yee?" She paused, then spoke again. "No way. I've known him since he was a kid, and he doesn't have a mean bone in him." More listening, then a deep sigh. "Yes, he's got a record. He was a good kid who had some issues with drugs, but I recently heard he was in school full-time, working part-time." She clicked keys. "Last arrest he was twenty. He's twenty-six now, and nothing but a speeding ticket since. He wouldn't send those emails, Delia."

I sat, keeping myself busy with work as I tried not to eavesdrop, but I assumed Eve would've asked me to leave if it was something I shouldn't hear, or she'd have taken the call in private.

A few minutes later, Eve hung up the phone. "Damn it."

"Was that about our mystery emailer?"

"Yeah. Isaiah and my son were joined at the hip until Derrick went off to the Naval Academy. I saw that boy almost every day for years, but then only while my son was home on breaks. When Derrick got deployed, I didn't see Isaiah for a few years. I do remember that his Grandmother Yee passed away around the time Derrick went to Iraq for the first time. She was Isaiah's rock and, when she died, he had a bit of a rough patch. But I saw him a few months ago, and he'd just started studying at the community college for network administration. He always was a smart kid, so I was glad to see him grounded again."

"So what makes anyone think he sent the emails?"

She frowned. "His computer experience, for one. And for two, they all go back to a single terminal at the library. A terminal several librarians remembered seeing him use more than once. Of course, a lot of other people have used it multiple times too, so it's speculation at this point."

I blinked. "But since he's studying network administration, wouldn't he use different computers in different places to make it harder to track him?"

Eve smiled, but it was more a baring of teeth than anything. "You would think so. And actually, Delia agrees. Also because the librarian who works days at the reference desk nearest the computers is one of Delia's friends and she remembers Isaiah, because he used to use the computers all the time, but she doesn't remember seeing him there in the last few months. My guess is he's using the computers at the college now, since he's in classes there. Anyway, Delia was just letting me know they had a suspect and they'd be interviewing him. She wasn't aware that I know him." She shifted her gaze to the clock on the wall and pushed up from her desk, squaring her shoulders. "Time for the briefing. We'll do that, and then I'll answer any other questions you have."

We headed to the briefing room together. My mind replayed the contents of those emails over and over again, and a shiver shook my body. I tried to hide it, but I'm pretty sure Eve caught my reaction. I couldn't help it. When I signed on to do this job, I'd never considered it might be dangerous. Oh, life in and of itself had dangers, but I hadn't put two and two together with cops and work and people hell-bent on retribution.

I had now.

Eve held out her hand and I preceded her into the room. It was full, standing room only. I looked over my shoulder at her, and she nodded to a place on the far side of the room where it was slightly less crowded. I wound my way over there, murmuring *excuse me* as people turned in my direction, their eyes curious.

I cursed under my breath. I knew what it was—a stranger in their midst—but I hated being the center of attention like that. When I got to the space big enough for both of us, I shrank back against the wall and tried to act like a piece of the furniture.

A man stepped to the podium and called for silence, nodding at Eve. I thought she was going up there, but instead she gave me a devilish grin, then spoke. "Before we get started, I'd like to introduce you all to Talia Wasserman, in case you haven't met her yet. She replaced Bev as my civilian assistant and will be working the festival with me and those of you who've volunteered to help over the course of the day."

Blood rushed to my cheeks, but I gave a small wave. "Hi?"

People laughed, then turned back to the podium and settled down.

I kept my voice low. "I know you're my boss, but expect payback when you least expect it."

Laughter danced in Eve's eyes. "Looking forward to it." The humor faded. "But seriously, it's important that everyone knows who you are, especially if anything goes wrong on Sunday."

My stomach turned over. I didn't have a response to that, so I just swallowed and nodded and refocused my attention on the speaker. Eve fleetingly laid a hand on my shoulder, then dropped it to her side.

We were there for about half an hour, and several people spoke. They shared the details of the emails Eve had received, and what little Delia had uncovered related to them. They also discussed the measures they'd be taking to ensure crowd safety as well as officer safety. After going over the duty schedule and the fielding questions from the officers in the audience, the man who'd opened the meeting—the deputy chief of police—ended it with a final few words.

"This warning appears to be directed specifically to our female officers. Everyone keep your eyes open and report all viable threats to them, or to anyone else." He paused to let the words sink in. "Dismissed."

I now had a giant knot in my gut, and my head reeled from all the information I'd just been given. As we walked back to our office, I asked one of the fifty questions I had, starting with the most innocuous one. "How do you—they—keep this all straight?"

Eve lifted a shoulder. "You learn to juggle a lot of balls at once. But there will be a few key people in a command vehicle with access to everyone's radios, to headquarters, to the state police. They'll be the ones keeping track of everything." She turned shrewd eyes to me. "What else?"

I jumped into the biggie, the one that had me most concerned. "Do you think there's a real chance of something happening?"

Her shoulder moved again. "Maybe. Not enough to cancel the event. Too much to not take extra precautions."

I sucked in a deep breath, let her easy confidence bolster my courage. "Okay. That . . . helps. If you don't mind, I'm going to head out a little early today to take care of a few things, since I'll be working on Sunday."

Eve dropped into her chair, pushing buttons on the phone, the receiver to her ear. "It's not like you don't give us an extra half hour or hour every day. Go for it. I'll see you Sunday." She held up one finger as she listened to a message, then dropped the phone into the cradle. "I almost forgot. You'll need this."

She stood and turned to the credenza behind her, leaning over as she bent to get something out of a drawer. I barely managed to lift my eyes from her ass when she straightened and tossed it at me.

Fear of getting caught ogling the boss made me slow to react, and I bobbled the pile of fabric that landed in my hands. A hot flush started in my chest and worked its way up. I had to clear my throat with a cough before I could speak. "What's this?"

"Got you a uniform shirt to wear to events where you represent the department. You probably want to wash it first because the dye runs if you get sweaty. Don't ask me how I know." She grimaced, shook her head. "But wear it Sunday so everyone knows you're part of the team, okay?"

"Okay."

Eve sat back down and sighed, grabbing a folder from the pile on her desk.

"Don't stay too late today. You need a break too." The second the words left my mouth I wanted to call them back. She was the boss, and I was the flunky, and what the hell was I doing telling her what to do?

Instead of giving me massive side-eye, she smiled. "Thanks for worrying. I'm good. Now go enjoy your Sabbath."

I'd shared my reasons for not working late Fridays and on Saturdays with Eve, and I appreciated her understanding. "Thanks. See you Sunday."

Chapter
FOUR

Sunday dawned clear and comfortably warm, never a given for mid-fall, but I was grateful. If I was going to be outside all day, I didn't want to freeze or sweat to death, and the expected sixty-five to seventy-degree weather was perfect for a street festival.

I ate a bigger breakfast than usual, because who knew when I'd get time to eat? I hoped I would, because this festival always had food samples from most of the restaurants in the area, and every year I looked forward to eating my way through them. I remembered the year Seth and I had ditched the girls, who'd thought it was boring, and made a date out of it. We'd been there all day and had practically rolled into bed that night, too full to do anything but snuggle. It was a good memory, but bittersweet, and I pushed it out of my head.

That was then, and Seth was gone. This was now.

I coated on a thick layer of sunscreen, then dressed in khakis and the police-department-emblazoned T-shirt Eve had given me. She hadn't been kidding about washing it first. The water in the washer had turned a deep blue, and I'd actually washed it a second time, because that dye on my fair skin would've turned me into a blueberry.

Unfortunately, since it was cotton, that second washing had made it shrink, so now the shirt was a little tighter than I normally liked to wear, but it would have to do.

I stuffed the things I'd need into a backpack, threw a light sweatshirt on, then locked up and headed out.

I parked in one of the decks and walked over to where Eve had told me we'd be set up, enjoying the sun on my face and the cool morning air. When I got there, she handed me a cup of coffee. "Here you go, addict."

"Mmmm," I said, grinning at her snark. I took a sip and let out a happy groan as the flavor hit my taste buds—pumpkin spice. Eve knew me well after several weeks. "Bless you."

She grinned back and lifted her cup of what had to be tea, because she *really* didn't do coffee at all. "We've got a locker inside the truck for personal stuff. You can drop your bag in there, but you might want to keep your phone and some money if you want to buy anything. It's going to be hard to get to it once we've got things up and going."

"Sounds good." I quickly stowed my belongings, and came back out of the truck, ready to get to work on my first public event for the department. Someone else had already erected a canopy next to the command truck and set up tables, but that was it. I sucked in a deep breath, then rubbed my hands together. "Okay, let's do this. What first?"

"I'm going to set up the fingerprinting station, if you want to get the tables ready. Only put half of the giveaways out. We'll save the rest for the afternoon crew."

"Sounds like a plan." I got everything arranged in a way I hoped made sense and stood back to admire my handiwork. Something seemed missing, but I couldn't remember what. Just as I opened my mouth to call Eve, someone grabbed my sweatshirt from behind and I let out a yelp that had my boss lifting her head, her eyes shooting daggers at the person behind me.

I spun, not knowing what to expect, but the heartbreakingly familiar face wasn't it. *Fair skin, reddish-brown hair and blue eyes, and the Wasserman nose.* "Noah!" I smacked him in the chest, frowned at him. "What are you doing here?"

He laughed, the sound twisting my heart. Seth's brother was built so much like him, laughed so much like him, *looked* so much like him that it often threw me, even this many years later. Not his fault that their family genes were so strong, but still.

Before he could answer, Eve was right beside me. "Everything okay?"

Noah pulled me close, kissing the side of my head as he held out a hand. "Noah Wasserman. Talia's brother-in-law."

Eve leveled a raised brow at him. "Do you make a habit of assaulting unsuspecting women, Mr. Wasserman?"

If I hadn't spent the last month and a half working for her and getting to know her, I would've thought she was serious, but I knew the nuances of her body language. She was playing with him . . . mostly . . . and fighting a grin.

Noah tensed and flushed. "I—"

"Yes, he does. All the time. I think you should lock him up." I smiled sweetly up at him, and he let out a low growl.

"Jeez, Talia. You've gotten mean."

"Wah, wah."

Eve's laugh broke free, and she held out her hand to shake Noah's. "Nice to meet you, but please—give a warning next time. Assault is a real threat for women."

"I know." And he did. The grin slid off Noah's face, leaving a hard edge behind. His wife had been sexually assaulted before they'd met, and occasionally the trauma of it still reared its head. "Point taken."

I bumped his hip with mine, trying to lighten the mood. "So what are you doing here?"

"All the electrical stuff for two of the blocks, including the stages."

I frowned. "Lila didn't mention anything about working today."

"That's because it was a last-minute thing, and she didn't know. The company scheduled to do it had a fire in their shop late yesterday afternoon. They lost half their stuff and needed some extra help, so we're doing two blocks for them and another small company is covering two blocks. By the way, your daughter has quite the vocabulary when being woken up at 6 a.m. on a weekend." He rolled his eyes, but they were warm with humor and love.

I couldn't hold back a laugh, because yeah, my daughter was sweet unless you woke her early. A morning person, she was not. And her repertoire of swear words had increased dramatically when she started working with mostly men. "Where do you think she learned those words, Uncle Noah?"

He winced. "Point."

Just then, my phone buzzed against my ass. I pulled it out, read the text from Lila.

Working at the festival today. Will find you if I manage to stay awake and Uncle Noah doesn't work us to death. YAWWWWWN. Early on the weekend is SO wrong even if it's time and a half.

I fought a laugh.

"Let me guess," Eve said. "Your daughter?"

"Yup. Grumpy about being up early on the weekend. Said she'd stop by later." I bumped Noah's hip again. "That is, if her tyrant of a boss gives her some free time."

Noah grinned wryly. "She'll take it whether I say yes or not."

"Hmmm. I wonder where she gets that stubborn streak from." I raised a brow in challenge.

"You," Eve said, deadpan.

"You," Noah agreed.

I had to laugh. "Busted." They weren't wrong. I used to tease Seth that Lila's stubbornness came from him, but the truth was, he'd been the easygoing one in our relationship. Standing on tiptoe, I kissed Noah's cheek. "I have to get back to work now, but I'll see you later."

He squeezed me once, nodded goodbye to Eve, and then left. I stared after him for several heartbeats, and jumped when Eve's voice landed next to my ear.

"You okay?"

"Yeah. My husband and Noah looked similar enough they were often mistaken for twins, even though they were three years apart. Sometimes when Noah surprises me like that, I just . . . forget." I rolled my shoulders, putting the past back where it belonged. I pointed at the table. "Anyway, I feel like I'm missing something here, and I can't figure out what it is."

Eve touched my arm lightly, and I saw a flash of sympathetic understanding in her eyes. Before I had a chance to ask her about it, she turned away, inclining her head and studying the things laid out in front of us.

We said the same thing at the same time. "The trifold backdrops."

We'd brought them into our office to do some repairs on them and I'd told Eve I'd put them back in the truck. "I'll head back to the station and grab them."

Eve shook her head. "No time. I need you here more than we need them. People are going to start showing up in the next fifteen minutes or so."

My stomach sank. "I am so sorry."

She lifted a shoulder. "If that is all that goes wrong today, we'll call this a success."

She might, but I wouldn't—*my first big event, and I fucked up?* I didn't have time to wallow in self-recrimination, though, because Eve hadn't been wrong. Within a few minutes, people started to arrive, and by the time we were half an hour in, it was a wall-to-wall sea of humanity.

The best part of the morning was all the really young kids happy to get police badges and meet the K-9 puppy. The worst part was watching Eve get verbally battered by cranky citizens who didn't think the police department did enough. She was far more collected than I would've been—I was only a bystander, and I wanted to scream.

After one particularly red-faced, irate older man stomped off, leaving our area clear for the first time in an hour, Eve came over and let out a sigh ripe with frustration.

"You okay?" I asked, the same thing she'd asked me earlier.

"Would you believe he wanted to know why I couldn't stop the next-door neighbors from playing in the cul-de-sac? Said the noise disturbed his peace." She deepened her voice. "*They're out there laughing and making noise and riding those bikes around for hours.* Christ. They're kids. That's what they should be doing. I don't get paid nearly enough to deal with people who think kids having fun is a crime."

In the blink of an eye, she wiped the frustration from her face as a small girl of four, maybe five, with big brown eyes, a head full of beaded braids, wearing a multicolored tutu and wings raced up to her. Eve smiled at her. "Can I help you?"

"Mama said you're a policeman," she said, the word coming out like *plisheman*.

Eve crouched in front of the little girl and tugged at a fairy wing. "Your mama's right. I *am* a police officer."

"Caleb said only boys can be plishemen."

Eve tugged again. "Caleb's wrong. Girls can become police officers too. Girls can be anything they want to be."

The girl cocked her head and studied Eve, then nearly knocked her over with a tackle hug. "I want to be a fairy-princess-doctor-plishoffer-astronaut-dancer."

I grinned at her exuberance and handed Eve one of the sticker badges we had.

"Be all those things, baby girl," Eve said, peeling the back of the sticker off and smoothing the badge on the girl's moon-phase shirt. "Any or all of them."

The girl's mother had a soft smile on her light-brown face. "See, Kiera. I told you you could."

"I know!" Kiera bounced up and down and twirled. "Can we go back to see the people with the telescope? I want to see the moon again!" She stopped bouncing and flung herself at a tall man who'd stopped beside her mother, hugging his legs. "Daddy!"

The man's dark-brown face creased into a smile that matched his wife's. He scooped his daughter up and settled her in his arms. She let out a gusty sigh that shook her whole small body, and laid her head against his shoulder, arms around his neck, eyes closed.

After saying they'd already had Kiera fingerprinted, they headed off.

"Pretty sure she's actually going to be all those things," I said to Eve. "Especially now that she can show her badge to Caleb."

"I hope so. I'm tired of hearing that girls can't do this or can't be that." Eve pointed to the left, where fairy princess Kiera was dancing in the street with kids from a performing arts school. "It's been so long since my son was little. I forgot how much energy they have. I wish I could bottle it up."

"Me too." I looked around and, at the risk of jinxing everything, said what I'd been thinking. "Rude old guy aside, today's gone well, huh?" As I waited for her to answer, I stripped off my sweatshirt. It had gotten warm, and I was roasting. When I turned back, Eve was watching me, her eyes on my too-tight shirt. A shiver slid down my spine, and I had a hard time hiding it.

Eve's gaze met mine, our eyes locking for a charged moment. She was the first to look away, and as I tried to get my heart back under control, I nearly missed her answer.

Her voice was husky. "It is, but I hate to break the bad news to you, rookie. It's only eleven."

That caught my attention, and I blinked. "Really? Only two hours?"

She laughed, cutting the tension. "Really. Community events like these are great, but time doesn't exactly fly."

Delia Butler came over then, handing us each an ice-cold bottle of water, which I took gratefully, for more than one reason. I unscrewed the cap and slugged back a few good swallows, noticing Eve doing the same. *So, not just me?* I wondered, then mentally snorted. Just because I was hot and bothered didn't mean Eve was too. And besides. *Boss. Still my boss.*

Delia was accompanied by a tall man with sun-streaked light-brown hair and fair skin who wore a wedding band and a watchful gaze. I'd seen that look before, and I would bet that he was also law enforcement of some kind. "Talia, this is my husband, Colin." She turned to him. "I told you about her—Eve's new assistant."

"Nice to meet you, Talia. I've heard good things."

"Same."

He turned to Eve. "Anything yet?"

"No. Are you working today?" Eve asked him. I must have looked puzzled because Eve added, "Colin works for the State Fire Marshal's office as an arson investigator."

Score one for me.

Colin scowled. "Not officially, no. But if you think I'm about to let my pregnant wi—"

Delia put her hand over his mouth. "You really don't want to go there today. I'm fine. This is what I'm trained for." When he gave her a *you've got to be kidding me* look, she dropped her hand to fiddle with the shamrock charm on a chain around her neck. "Please?"

I understood exactly where Colin was coming from, even though I got Delia's side as well. It had taken everything I had not to tell Lila to go home, just in case something bad happened, but the truth of the matter was, we couldn't protect those we loved every moment of every day. I'd learned that the hard way, that sometimes the terrible things came when you were least expecting them. Like arguing with your husband, then grudgingly kissing him goodbye and sending him off to work, promising to talk things out later—and losing him to an aneurysm that same day. If I let it rule me, I'd never let my girls out of my sight.

Eve cleared her throat. "We agreed you'd only be eyes on the crowd today, Dee. Especially since you're still on limited duty, and whoever this is seems to have issues with female cops."

Delia flushed, her pale cheeks almost the same red as her hair, but Colin grinned. "I knew I liked you, Poe." He slung his arm over Delia's shoulder but winced when she pinched his side. "Come on, brat. My son needs food, anyway."

"Daughter."

His eyes remained cop-sharp as they continued to scan the crowd. "We'll see."

Delia allowed him to pull her along, but called out over her shoulder. "Keep me posted."

Eve watched them walk away, then sighed. "I'd feel better if she was off altogether, but you can't take the cop out of the woman."

"I'd imagine not." I was going to ask her if she was ever able to be just Eve, but we were hit with another wave of people stopping by. The traffic was steady for almost an hour, and I decided the next time we had a break, I'd see about grabbing some lunch for both of us, then trying to find Lila so I could introduce her to Eve.

"Miz Poe?"

Eve turned slowly toward the young man who'd come around the side of the truck. He was tall and slender, with brown skin, straight black hair and dark eyes. I recognized him from the photo Eve had shown me.

"Isaiah," Eve said, her voice even.

He frowned at her, but didn't seem angry. Maybe . . . lost? "Why'd you let them bring me in like that? You could've just asked me."

She held her hand out toward the truck, pointing to where he'd just come from. Out of the way of foot traffic, out of the public eye. "Let's go talk. Talia, keep an eye on things for me, okay?"

My heart jammed my throat. "Will do."

And they walked out of my sight.

Chapter FIVE

Someone must've called for backup, because it didn't take long for two officers to make their way to the command truck and our booth. I recognized OFC Ramirez of the embarrassing first-day-of-work metal-detector incident. When he looked around, I silently pointed back toward the sidewalk where Eve and Isaiah had gone, and he motioned for me to stay where I was.

I did.

The other officer, one I didn't recognize, stayed with me as Ramirez headed behind the truck. Blonde and petite, OFC Anderson didn't look like she could stop a child, but after working with the police department for the last several weeks, I knew better than to be misled by appearances.

"Any issues yet?" I asked her.

Anderson shook her head. "Nothing that fits the warning." She helped me with the people coming by, and it felt like hours until Eve reappeared in the break between the truck and the next booth, still on the sidewalk.

Isaiah Yee was at her side, talking and gesturing with his hands. Ramirez had a small notebook out and was jotting things in it. He spoke into the radio on his shoulder, then wrote something else down. Eve made a reply I couldn't hear, and Ramirez nodded and came back our way.

Eve put her hand on Isaiah's arm and talked to him, leaning close. The conversation looked intense, and when he shrugged her arm off and stalked away, her shoulders slumped for a long moment before she purposely straightened as though drawing on the mantle of command. My heart twisted for her, and I wondered who she vented to, who held her close when the stresses of work got to be too much.

Everyone needed someone.

Back at our booth, she took over from Anderson, who went back out to patrol, and began handing out fliers like nothing had happened.

"Eve?"

She shook her head infinitesimally. "Not right now, okay?"

"Sure." She was the boss, so she was in charge, and she didn't owe me any explanations about an active case—or her feelings. For the next hour, I helped with fingerprints while she spoke with people who stopped by for information and just to talk to a cop. Finally, two officers came to relieve us so we could grab food. I hesitated. "Want to walk with me?"

She rubbed her hand over her forehead and winced.

My stomach flip-flopped, but I covered it with a faint smile. "Okay. I'll be back as soon as I can."

I started to walk away when Eve called out.

"Wait, Talia."

I waited. When she caught up, she directed us up to the sidewalk, behind the booths, where the foot traffic was far less and we could walk side by side.

She spoke first. "Isaiah said he didn't send the emails, but after Dee interviewed him, he asked around. It was one of the homeless men who use the computers at the library. Apparently the notes were meant as a warning. He heard a guy talking about how he wants to teach female cops a lesson. No real specifics. I'll find a way to meet with him without letting him know Isaiah told us."

"That's good, right?"

"Yes and no. Good it's unlikely Isaiah is involved. Bad he feels like I betrayed him. Also bad that we're back to square one." She grimaced. "And I hesitated about leaving with you because I didn't want to draw attention to you by virtue of walking with a female cop, even if the threat is an unknown one at this time."

I rolled my eyes and pointed at my police department shirt. "Uh, Eve? If anyone's been checking things out, they've already seen me with cops, male and female."

She lifted a shoulder. "True."

"And you have to eat. But you hate to eat alone."

A smile quirked the corner of her mouth. "Also true. Someone has been paying attention."

Hopefully she didn't realize just how much attention, because that would be awkward. "I work for a cop, you know. I've learned things."

This time, she gave an out-and-out laugh. "All right, Ms. Smart-ass. We'll go find some food."

We headed back into the street and walked in companionable silence, talking only to discuss our options, debating between Indian, Mexican, Irish, standard American hamburgers and hot dogs, Jamaican, Chinese, Italian, and Greek.

I decided on jerk chicken from the Jamaican place, and Eve went for a gyro. We carried our food to an open spot near one of the stages and settled onto the curb, watching the people go by. "Looks like a good crowd," I said.

Eve nodded. "And behaving themselves too. Only one arrest? That has to be a record. Of course, we still have a few hours to go."

We ate a few bites in silence. I looked around for Lila or Noah, which reminded me . . . "Earlier today, when I told you about Noah resembling Seth, it seemed like you understood how I felt. Personally, I mean." I hesitated when she slid a raised-brow glance my way. "Ugh, never mind. I'm being nosy, and it's none of my business. It's a fault of mine."

"I've been known to be nosy myself. Hazard of the job." She studied me for a moment before staring down at the ground, which was so unlike the Eve I'd grown to know that warning bells went off in my head. "My son looks a lot like his father did at that age. And sometimes it's startling and painful even though Trey's been gone for over twenty years. So yeah. I get it."

My heart stuttered at the unexpected revelation. "I'm sorry."

"It's been a really long time. He was a Marine killed in a helicopter crash while deployed." She lifted a shoulder, let it drop. "I don't talk about him much."

Oh, no. "I shouldn't have brought it up. Especially today, with everything else going on." I wished I'd kept my mouth shut. "I'm so sorry."

"Don't be. I'm the one who started in with the questions earlier, anyway." Her smile was faint, but a genuine thread of amusement underlined her words. "And hey, now that you know? Please smack me in the head whenever I start freaking out because I haven't heard from Derrick. Deal?"

I laughed, as I'm sure she'd intended. "Deal."

She took another bite of her almost-gone gyro, and some of the tzatziki sauce got smeared on her cheek. She kept eating, as though she hadn't noticed.

I'm not sure what the hell got into me, but I lifted my hand toward her face. "You have something here," I said, wiping at it with my thumb.

She froze, and so did I.

I dropped my hand, let out a strangled sound, and, setting my food on the ground beside me, bent over to hide my flaming face.

"Talia?"

I kept my head in my lap. "Don't ask. I don't ... I'm sorry. Motherly instinct?" *Liar liar*, my conscience taunted, but I shushed it.

She didn't respond, and I turned my head slightly, my breath catching. Surely that wasn't *disappointment* in her eyes? "It's fine," she said, her voice far milder than it usually was, as though she had to work at keeping it level. "You just surprised me."

"Me too," I muttered under my breath. I picked my food back up and focused on stuffing my mouth, hoping to keep my foot out of it.

Er, *again*.

Luckily, the public kept me from making a fool of myself. Eve had a steady stream of people stopping to talk with her. She seemed to know many of them, though not all. And when they talked, she listened. Not casually, but deeply, as though their thoughts were important to her. She'd made an indelible mark as the head of Community Relations, and it showed.

I ate and watched and listened and enjoyed, at the same time keeping my eyes opened for Lila. Up on the stage, teens were performing a number from *Hamilton* and on the ground behind the stage, I saw a flash of a blonde ponytail hanging down over a dark-green T-shirt, which was the color Noah used for the company. She disappeared from my sight, then came out on the other side with her ever-present backpack slung over her shoulder. When she got to the front of the stage, she glanced left and right and then started off in the opposite direction from where we were sitting.

"Lila!"

At her name, she turned. She looked around but didn't seem to see me, so I stood, waving. Her face lit up, and my heart went to mush. Nothing like knowing one of your babies was happy to see you.

I gave her a tight hug and she squeezed back. "How's your day going?"

"I've been hit on three times, and two of those times, the guys also told me women shouldn't do electrical work. I told them to fuck off." She wrinkled her nose. "So, yeah, that happened. How's your day going?"

I tugged her ponytail. "Language, please."

Lila rolled her eyes. "Mom. Even *you* say fuck."

She wasn't wrong about that. "I'm your mother."

"I'm almost twenty-four. *And* I pay my own bills. Pretty sure I'm old enough."

A soft snort behind me had me looking over my shoulder.

Eve rose and joined us. "I see the snarky apple doesn't fall far from the snarky tree."

I grinned. She wasn't wrong, either. "Eve, this is my daughter Lila. Lila, this is my boss, Lieutenant Eve Poe."

"Nice to meet you, Lieutenant Poe." Lila's eyes twinkled and I knew I was in trouble. She rocked back on her heels and smiled. "So, what embarrassing thing should I tell you about my mother?" She tapped a finger on her cheek. "Oh, I know. There was this one time when—"

"Lila!"

Eve laughed. "Nice to meet you too. And while I'd love to hear all the details, I'm going to be a mean boss. Your mom and I need to get back to the booth, and if I'm not mistaken, that's *your* boss headed this way."

Lila gave in with a sunny grin. "I'm sure I'll get another chance. You should come over for Shabbat dinner one Friday. Mom's a really good cook, and she makes the best challah."

"I'd enjoy that," Eve said.

My stomach flipped, even as my mind whirled off into places it had no business going. *Eve in my house? And once Lila went home? Then what?* As I'd done ruthlessly over and over these past several weeks, I shoved the thoughts back.

I squeezed my girl again. "What time are you done?"

"Two. I'm going to meet Tee and Yas and we'll grab some food before the restaurants pack everything up. Then I think we're headed to the movies. I'll text you later. Love you, Mom."

"Love you too, baby."

My mind wavered between thoughts of my daughter and of the woman by my side as Eve and I headed back to the booth and relieved the officers who'd covered for us. She disappeared inside the command truck, then came to the door with the second half of the giveaways we'd held back. I took them with a murmured thanks, and she ducked back inside. I filled the table again, and handed things out as people came by.

Eve was in the truck for about ten minutes, and I could hear the low murmur of her voice. It sounded like she was on the phone, and I assumed she was either filling someone in about what she'd learned or getting more information.

When she came out, she looked pensive and somewhat remote. I wasn't sure if it was because of the discussion we'd had about Derrick's father, the fact that I'd touched her when I shouldn't have, or if it was something work related, but for the rest of the afternoon, there was an awkward silence in the lull between people stopping by our booth, and I didn't like it. In the morning as we'd set up, we'd talked about everything under the sun. Our kids. The changes over the last twenty years in the city we called home. The latest twists in the television show we both loved.

Everything but the tension that seemed to simmer between us.

It didn't feel one-sided, but maybe I was wrong. Maybe I was just seeing what I wanted to see. I still didn't know if Eve was in a relationship. I didn't think so, because we'd talked about family enough. I knew she had two sisters and a brother she'd said was spoiled rotten because he was the baby and the only boy. Her parents were in their seventies, both in good health and now living in South Carolina, near her oldest sister and family. Her younger sister and her brother still lived here, and she saw them often.

But, other than the fact that she'd said "*it's no wonder I only date women*," I couldn't remember hearing her talk about someone special in her life.

The burgeoning feelings I had for Eve reminded me of when I'd first met Seth. A fluttering in my stomach. A desire to spend time with her, to learn more about what made her tick. Their differences aside, the feelings I had for each affected me in the same way, a way that solidified my understanding of my own sexuality and what attracted me to someone. It wasn't their gender, but that indefinable *something* that drew me like a magnet.

I loved the way Eve truly liked and cared about other people. A high school principal, Seth had been the same. When he'd talked about his teachers and students, it had been obvious how much they meant to him. Family had been important to him too. The girls and I had been his world, but he'd stayed close with his brother, the two of them thick as thieves. Eve was also close to her family. I knew how hard it was to have her son overseas in a war zone, and she depended on her sisters and brother to help keep her sane.

Other than that, they were very different people. Clearly, you liked who you liked and it truly was indefinable. But I no longer had *any* doubts that I could feel the same sexual feelings for a woman as I did for a man.

For *this* woman, at least.

I'd made a grave mistake earlier, touching her cheek, feeling the softness of her skin. Now that I knew how silky it was, I wanted to revel in the sensations, to rub my own cheek against hers. I wanted my lips on hers, and I wanted to taste the salt on her skin along her jaw and her neck.

The problem was I still didn't know if she felt the same way. Or if a relationship would even be allowed, given our work dynamic as boss and subordinate.

Annnd . . . I really needed to stop thinking about that, because the ache between my thighs—and in my heart—was growing.

The street festival officially finished at five, but by four thirty, traffic had dwindled down to almost nothing. We started packing things up, taking down the canopy and the tables and stowing them inside the truck. We worked in near silence until we were done.

"Good job today," Eve said, though her usual smile was missing. "I'm driving the truck back to the station, so you're free to head out. And come in late tomorrow, since we were here all day. The work will wait."

My heart sank at her remoteness. "Thanks." I grabbed my backpack and my sweatshirt out of the storage locker and turned to go. I was at the door, my foot ready to go down onto one step when I glanced over my shoulder.

That *look* was back on Eve's face, but as soon as I turned to her she wiped it off. I'd seen it, though. Part pensive, part longing, part something I couldn't name. "Are you okay?"

She waved me off. "Just tired. Thanks again. Be careful going home."

I frowned but let the obvious lie slide. I wanted to make her tell me, so I could ease whatever was bothering her, and wasn't that a kick? And I wanted to ask the question that was eating at me, but I couldn't do it. Didn't have the chutzpah to bare my soul and potentially make working at the job I'd come to love uncomfortable and awkward—for both of us. Instead, I nodded. "Have a good night, Eve."

At home, I took a shower to wash off the sweat of the day, groaning out loud when I realized my two washes hadn't completely cleared the dye from the shirt. The tops of my breasts bore a slash of blueberry, as did the insides of my arms.

Lovely.

I fell face-first onto my bed, buck naked, and dozed for about forty-five minutes. When I woke, I threw on one of Seth's now threadbare T-shirts over panties, then went to the kitchen and fixed myself a plate of fruit, cheese, and crackers. I curled up on the sofa in the family room with a glass of wine in one hand and the television remote in the other. I was an episode behind in the show Eve and I both watched and loved to debate, and I'd begged her not to spoil it for me. She'd teasingly given me a week to catch up.

About twenty minutes into it, I got up to get a glass of water and saw the message light blinking on my cell phone. I thumbed it awake and saw a text from Lila—*running late to the movie, will catch up with you tomorrow*—and a call from a local number I didn't recognize. I'd been getting spam calls for the last few months, so I ignored it and went back to watch the rest of the episode.

Before my ass even hit the sofa cushion, the doorbell rang, and I glanced at the clock. It was just past seven, and I frowned. Lila would use her own key, and no one else came calling on Sunday nights.

I was going to ignore it, but then a knock came.

"You there, Talia? It's Eve."

Chapter SIX

I opened the door, heedless of my lack of real clothing. "Are you okay? What's wrong?"

"What *isn't* wrong?" Eve gave a little half laugh loaded with self-derision. "I have a son who's engaged to a woman I've never met. I have a citizen who possibly wants to do harm to women in blue, or maybe just wants us spinning our wheels. Then there's . . ."

Her voice drifted off and, still concerned, I stepped back and motioned her in. After closing the door behind her, I led her to the kitchen. I didn't question the impulse, though I probably should've. Guests were entertained in the living room. Family by blood and by fire hung out in my somewhat messy kitchen.

She took in the controlled chaos in a trained cop's glance that missed nothing, then plopped into a chair at the scarred wooden table, dropping her head into her hands.

I was so used to seeing Eve in a professional capacity—and rarely speechless—that this threw me. In case she needed it, I gave her a moment to gather her thoughts, putting on water for tea. I found a box of various herbal blends on the top shelf of the cupboard where I kept things I rarely used, but had to stand on tiptoe to get it. When I turned back, she was watching me, her focus intent, her eyes sharp.

I blinked. "What?"

"I am losing my damn mind," she muttered, looking away. "That's the only acceptable possibility."

I raised a brow but said nothing.

She spoke quickly as though she'd change her mind if she didn't. "I can't ask this at work without risking someone overhearing and opening a sexual harassment complaint. Are you . . .? Do you . . .? *Christ.* I can't even get the damn words out." She dropped her head again.

My heart stuttered. Knowing this was a bad idea but suddenly past caring, I sat next to her. "Eve?"

I laid a hand on her arm, sucking in a breath at the charge that ran through me with that simple contact. Her eyes flew to mine, and in them I saw the same awareness I felt—intermingled with concern and confusion. On a shudder, I took a leap and let the words fly. "You want to know if you're the only one who feels this . . . connection?"

"Yeah."

I swallowed back my fear, because I couldn't make her do this alone. "Nope."

Her eyes widened slightly, and the tiniest of smiles quirked the corner of her mouth. "You're braver than I am."

That made me laugh, even as my pulse thudded erratically. "Yeah, not so much."

Her smile faded. "Knowing it is one thing. Doing something about it . . . This could be all kinds of bad."

That was the understatement of the century. "Because you're my boss."

"That's one reason."

"I can give you another." This might kill any chance we had before it even started, but she needed to know. "I, uh . . . I have no experience with this."

She nodded. "You haven't been with anyone since your husband."

"That too?"

Comprehension dawned in her eyes, along with wariness. "Oh. Are you sure you're bi?"

"Pretty sure." I got up and went over to the kettle, which was whistling madly. I turned it off, filled a mug with water, and brought the box of tea bags to the table. "Sorry. It's all I've got."

"It's fine."

While she chose a flavor, she didn't say anything else, and I understood her concern. Who wanted to bare their heart if the other person might realize they really weren't sure? I mean, there were no guarantees things would work between us—I'd told the girls many times that a relationship was always a risk—but whether or not I could handle a same-sex attraction added another layer. I took a deep breath and brain-dumped everything I'd been thinking about nearly nonstop since I'd learned who I'd be working for.

"When I was twelve, a friend and I found her dad's porn stash. She was all about the guys, but I remember looking mostly at the women. When I was in high school, I was confused because I had feelings for boys *and* girls." It had been terrifying, because I hadn't known anyone who'd liked someone of the same gender. "I was too busy to date, anyway, but you know how it was then." Eve nodded, so I continued. "When I came home after graduation without a boyfriend, my sister joked maybe I was a lesbian, but it didn't feel right, because I *knew* I liked guys. And then I met Seth, and everything was perfect. The fact that I might like women too didn't matter, because I was happy."

"So that's what makes you pretty sure?" Eve asked, her voice carefully measured. Protecting herself, maybe.

"Sort of. It's not just that, though." At her startled glance, I forged ahead. In for a penny, in for a pound. "It's you, Eve. I've been attracted to other women over the years, and I can't deny how you make me feel. Fifteen years ago, and six weeks ago, I felt the same way. Restless and itchy and—"

This time, she cut me off, leaning forward in the chair. "Aware," she said, the word thick with emotion.

"Yeah."

She tilted her head, studied me for a long moment. "So if anything were to happen between us, it would be what? Fulfilling a curiosity? Or a fantasy?"

It took a lot to anger me, but this totally pissed me off. "Fuck, no," I said through clenched teeth, proving that my daughter was right and I did drop the F-bomb when necessary. "And it's insulting you'd even ask. You know me better than that. I never intended to tell you how I feel, because I work for you and that's just awkward." I lashed out, knowing I shouldn't say the words even before they came out of my mouth. "*You're* the one who came here and opened the can of worms."

Her own temper flashed. I'd only seen it once before, the day she'd been pissed off with her son. "Because we're too old to be playing games, and I'm your goddamn boss, that's why. You touched me today and you've been walking on eggshells around me since the first day of work. And I needed to know *why* before I maybe wreck my whole fucking career on a woman who might only want a fling."

"I *told* you that you had something on your cheek."

"Bullshit."

We each sat back, arms crossed, glaring at each other, and the absurdity of it hit me. I *liked* this woman, *wanted* this woman, though at this very instant I wanted to strangle her. But we were arguing over liking each other too much? Talk about stupid. Had I learned nothing in twenty-plus years of marriage?

Apparently not.

I shoved up from the chair and got myself a drink of water—and some space—then leaned my ass against the counter.

Eve shoved to her feet, and my incredibly confused and frustrated and, yes, horny heart ached. She was *leaving*?

But instead of walking out the door, she strode forward, not stopping until she stood mere inches from me. Her voice came low and husky, and it echoed my earlier thoughts. "This is ridiculous."

"So, what now?"

"We forget this ever happened, and go back to the way things were?" she asked, getting impossibly closer.

I nodded, but my stomach ached. Nothing hurt more right now than the thought of lost possibilities.

"Bullshit," she said again, and then she cupped my cheek, rubbing her thumb against it. "That's what it felt like. Did your heart speed up? Your mouth go dry?"

I licked my lips, my eyes locked on hers as I nodded again.

"Oh, fuck me." She leaned forward, hand still on my cheek, and pressed her lips against mine, softly, giving me a chance to protest though I didn't think I had the breath to speak. When I didn't, she deepened the kiss, and the bottom dropped out of my stomach.

And my world.

I groaned low in my throat and she angled closer, bringing her body up against mine, her other hand sliding to my hip. As she rubbed small circles there, I opened my mouth on a gasp and her tongue touched mine.

My hands went up and I grabbed at her hips. She straddled my feet and her breasts brushed mine, causing her to jerk and me to make a needy moan. She tasted like apples and cinnamon, and I'd never smell that scent again without thinking of her.

Her mouth moved off mine and I would've complained except she began kissing and licking and biting and sucking along my jaw and neck and, *fuck*, that felt amazing.

I froze for one breath. This was the first intimate contact I'd had since Seth's death, but I knew deep in my heart he wouldn't have wanted me to remain celibate forever. It helped that Eve's kisses were so very different from his, that her lips were smooth and her skin smoother, that she didn't take but coaxed. Taking had its place, but good lord, this was amazing.

And now that I knew, I wanted more.

"You okay?" Eve asked warily.

"Mmm. But it's my turn," I murmured, taking her hand and leading her to the semi-dark family room. In the light from the muted television, her beautiful brown eyes carried a ring of amber around the edges that I hadn't seen before. And her body fairly vibrated with tension. I pulled her onto the sofa with me, then slid my hand behind her neck and tugged her close for another kiss. I didn't want her to think it was one-sided, that I was just allowing things to happen.

I wanted to let her know I wanted this, enough to take the lead.

We bumped noses and I laughed, but that laugh turned into a groan when the hand she didn't have clenched into a fist—yeah, I'd seen that—landed on my hip again, this time on bare skin. Her fingers danced against the edge of my panties along my hip.

When I came up for air, her voice was husky. "These should be illegal."

I looked down and felt myself turn brick red. "I need to do laundry."

Though a fairly modest cut, they were see-through and tied with ribbons on the side, and I'd bought them as a treat for myself, even though I'd figured only I would ever see them.

"I'm not complaining." Her hand moved up and her fingers grazed my ribs. "I got to see the back view when you were getting tea."

I sucked in a breath at that but didn't stop my own exploring. I unzipped the jacket she wore, knowing she favored sports bras under them if she was running, wanting to get my hands on her skin. To my shock, she didn't have a bra on, just a thin ribbed tank that did nothing to hide her aroused nipples.

My voice strangled in my throat.

She laughed softly. "I grabbed whatever was close. I decided if I didn't leave right then, I wouldn't."

I put my hand on her torso, curling it around her side. "I'm glad you did."

"Same." Her fingers clenched against my skin, her knuckles brushing against the underside of my bra-free breasts.

The ache between my thighs grew, and though we were both more than of age, assuaging that ache might be taking things a bit too far for a tentative first time together. That level of intimacy was a huge step.

Still, I wanted to touch her. Needed to. Allowing her time to say no, I slid my hand between us, up and under her shirt. I stopped at a thick, ridged line that marred the smoothness of her skin.

"Knife wound from when I worked patrol," Eve said. This time, it was my fingers that clenched, and my throat grew tight. She rubbed her cheek against mine. "It was a long time ago, Tal. And I'm rarely on the street anymore, not that it couldn't happen. Risks of the job. Not much I can do to change that."

My heart flipped over, and not just because of worry, though worry I did. The way she'd said my name was full of intimate affection and, at that moment, I realized that I could hurt her as much as she could hurt me. But I still didn't want to stop. "I know."

I withdrew my hand from under her shirt and she made a small whine of protest. I smiled, then broke free from her touch—only to gently guide her so she was lying on the sofa. Understanding dawned in her eyes, and she lifted her arms up over her head, tucking her hands beneath it. "Go for it," she drawled, her voice husky.

It was a wide sofa, so there was room for me to kneel beside her. I did, pushing her shirt up over her flat stomach. "You are in such good shape," I murmured, gliding my knuckles over the scar that seemed far, far too close to vital organs. "I probably shouldn't tell you this, but that first day you asked me if I wanted to join you? My brain went right to *in the shower*."

She groaned. "I know it did. It was all over your face. I thought for sure you'd turn around and never come back. I've never been one to spew sexual innuendo, but I can't seem to help it around you."

"Not even close. I wanted to join you there, to see if you were as sexy under your clothes as you looked." I leaned over and kissed the scar, then grinned up at her. "And you know that's just a dare, right? I'm going to be leaving things wide, wide open now."

A strangled laugh. "You're a dangerous, devious woman."

"Thank you."

She laughed again, but it choked off as I followed long-buried desires and put my tongue on her, licking around her belly button, then sucking gently at the soft curve of her hip. "You always smell like apples and cinnamon. I like it."

"Good to know." She shifted her hips and I realized I wasn't the only one who was fighting the ache of arousal.

I shoved her shirt up further, baring her breasts to my gaze, and my breath caught. They were small, but what she had was lovely. Firm, smooth, her pebbled nipples a darker brown than her skin. I glanced up at her face and hid a satisfied grin. Her jaw was tight, as though she had to force herself to stay still.

"Can I touch you?" I asked, my voice deeper than usual. I wanted this more than anything I'd wanted in a long time.

"I'll kill you if you don't put your hands on me right now."

I hadn't meant with my hands. I cupped her breast with my fingers while sucking her nipple into my mouth, hard, just the way I liked it.

She nearly bowed off the sofa. "*Jesus*, Tal. Warn a girl." When I sucked again, she groaned. "And you say you've never done this before? God help me."

I laughed, then shifted so I was stretched out beside her, one leg draped over hers. "Another dare." I played with one firm breast and licked the other while she squirmed beneath me.

And then she turned the tables, though she never moved her hands. She drew her leg up until her thigh pressed against my core. I gasped, and her nipple popped from between my lips. She pressed harder with her thigh, just enough to move my body closer so she could claim my lips. "My turn."

Even though I had probably fifty pounds on her, she managed to get me under her while she straddled my legs. Her top was still pushed above her breasts, and while I watched, my breathing ragged, she stripped off both the open jacket and the tank. The real beauty of her paled against the fantasy in my mind, and I liked the reality so much better. Strong, confident, sexy as hell. Her skin glowed wet where my mouth had been, and I reached out to touch.

"No, ma'am. You keep those dangerous hands to yourself. I want to play." She put her hands on the bottom of my T-shirt—my late husband's T-shirt—and stilled. I didn't know if I'd flinched or if she'd seen the sudden realization in my eyes. "You okay?"

"Yeah. I'm sorry. You're the first—" I tried again. "This is the first time I've been with anyone since Seth died. This was his shirt." It sounded so stupid when I said it, but her eyes softened.

"Why don't *you* take it off?" She leaned back and I did, dropping it over the edge of the sofa. She caressed my face lightly. "He's part of your life, and you don't want me touching that part of it. I understand."

I shook my head. "He's part of my history. You're part of my life. It's not that I don't want you to touch a stupid shirt. It's because I don't want you to feel like you're competing with him. You're not. I've had years to come to grips with the fact that he's gone. But this is still my first time in a very, very long time."

A tiny smile, and then she kissed me, ever so sweet. "I'll be gentle."

"I hope not *too* gentle."

A delicately arched eyebrow rose. "Challenge accepted."

I laughed, but it came out half snort, which made Eve laugh. You'd have thought we were in our teens instead of our fifties. Instead of ruining the moment, it made me even more comfortable with her and the fact that I was lying on my sofa, mostly naked with my *boss*, for fuck's sake, totally winging it. I mean, I'd watched lesbian porn, so I knew what went where and how things worked, but I hadn't figured out yet how *I* did things.

Or what turned Eve on.

I was looking forward to finding out.

And I wouldn't worry about the boss part right now, though. *Much*.

Eve kissed me on my sternum, between my breasts, then cupped them and pushed them together, paying attention to one nipple and then the other. My hips bucked under her and I choked back a needy groan—or tried to.

"Just getting started, Tal. Best thing about being with a woman is that we're not one and done. I can—*you* can—do this All. Night. Long."

I hadn't really considered that, but it did sound like a bonus. There had been nights with Seth that I'd barely gotten warmed up and he'd been at the finish line. Not often, because he'd been a generous, considerate lover, but it had happened.

I reached up because I *had* to touch Eve, had to get my hands on her tempting breasts right now, but lights bounced through the windows—which meant someone was pulling into the driveway.

I froze.

Chapter
SEVEN

Faster than I could imagine, Eve slid off the sofa, tossed me my shirt, and put her own shirt back on. Thank goodness *she* was thinking, since my lust-fogged brain hadn't caught up yet. Especially since the next thing I heard was a key in the lock.

Lila.

"Mom?"

That got me moving, and I tugged my shirt over my head with a grimace. "Don't you go anywhere," I whispered to Eve and pointed to the far side of the sofa. I took a steadying breath, let it out. "I'm in the family room, honey."

My daughter hesitated in the doorway. "Why are you sitting in the dark?"

"We were watching television."

There was a pregnant pause as my daughter weighed my words. "We?" She stepped into the room, then saw Eve on the sofa, and relaxed. "Oh, hey. Hi, Lieutenant Poe."

Eve smiled, but her voice was the tiniest bit unsteady. "Hi, Lila. You can call me Eve."

"Mom, can I talk to you for a minute?"

My eldest daughter was twisting the hem of her shirt and worrying her lip. I turned back to Eve and handed her the remote. "Excuse us?" After she nodded, Lila and I went into the kitchen. "What's wrong?" I asked her.

"Ryan was sitting on my steps tonight when I got back from the movies. He told me he made a mistake and he wants to get back together. He said he's missed me these last few weeks and he'll never cheat again."

My gut instinct was to tell her *oh, hell no*, but that wasn't a decision I could make for her. "What do you think?"

Her eyes swam. "I don't *know*. Tee and Yas both said no way. But I miss him too. He can change, right?"

I squeezed her hand even as my heart broke for her. "I honestly don't know what to tell you. I don't have any personal experience, and I don't know Ryan like you do. I've heard some women say, yes, men who've cheated can change. I've heard others say if they do it once, they'll do it again."

She let out a hiccupping sob. "That doesn't help."

"I'm sorry, honey. Do *you* think he can change? Knowing what you know of him, do you think he's capable of staying faithful? And, more importantly, knowing how you felt when you found out he cheated, can you go through this a second time if he can't?"

"Ugh. I just have to figure it out, don't I?"

"Yep. Sometimes adulting really sucks, I know." I opened my arms and pulled her in for a hug. "Why don't you think it over and we can talk after you sleep on it. Whatever you choose, I wouldn't do it tonight or even this week. If you decide to give him another chance, letting him sit and stew for a bit wouldn't be out of turn."

She laughed a watery laugh, and then froze.

"*Mom.* Is that a hickey on your neck?" Her eyes flew wide as she stared at me as though she'd never seen me before.

I moved to the hall bathroom to look in the mirror and flinched. Oy. And my hair was wild, my color high, and I looked like I'd been almost-fucked. *Busted.* "Maybe?"

She took in my T-shirt and bare legs, and color rose in her cheeks. My daughter wasn't a stupid woman, and her mouth opened and closed as she glanced from a half-dressed me to the door into the family room. Speechless, which I could honestly say wasn't a state that was natural to her. Another long beat of silence, and then just two words. "Your *boss?*"

"Maybe?"

Lila looked aghast, and my stomach twisted, but she surprised me. "I hope you know what you're doing, Mom. You always told us it's a bad idea to fish in the office pond."

Not a word about the fact that Eve was a woman. Not a single one, which warmed my heart and made my stomach unknot. "Sometimes, things just happen."

Lila rolled her eyes. "Like you'd *ever* let us get away with that."

She wasn't wrong, but to be honest, I wasn't sure where this was going so I didn't know what to say. A snort came from behind me, and I turned my head. My heart fluttered. *Eve.*

"Is everything okay?" she asked, leaning against the door frame.

My daughter glared at her. "You're her boss. How's that going to work?"

"Lila Mae Wasserman," I chided. "Watch your tone of voice, please."

To her credit, Eve didn't seem thrown by the question or the tone. "There are ways around it if your mother and I date. She can report to another officer but still work in our office. I can request a transfer. There's time to figure that out." She came into the kitchen, standing against the counter next to me, our bodies close but not touching. "This is all very new, and you're going to want to talk to your mom about it. I need to head home, anyway—I have an early meeting." She squeezed my hand, and that was all the warning I got.

My stomach did a slow roll when she leaned in, brushing a soft, lingering kiss over my lips while rubbing a thumb over my cheek. It was both sweet and erotic and I was nearly brought to my knees by it. Then she left and I stood there, shocked into silence, staring after her with my heart racing.

"Um, wow. That was . . . wow." Lila blinked at me, then to the door where Eve had exited. "You really like her?"

"I really like her." And because I felt like she needed to hear it, I kept going. "Your father's been gone a long time. And I don't think he'd want me to be alone forever, you know?"

She sighed but gave me a hug. "I know. I just . . . it's hard seeing you with someone besides Daddy." She furrowed her brow. "I didn't know you were bi."

Releasing her, I went to the fridge for some ice-cold water. "Do you honestly want to talk about my sexual orientation?"

She wrinkled her nose. "Maybe not in detail. I mean, I know you've *had* sex because Rissa and I are here, and you and Daddy weren't always quiet, anyway. But I didn't know you liked women too."

Blood drained from my face. "Excuse me? You heard us?"

She laughed. "Mom, really? I was a teenager. You didn't actually think I was asleep by eleven, did you?"

I buried my face in my hands.

"Rissa and I saw you argue and we heard you make up. Not such a terrible thing," she said, sounding a lot like her Yiddish-speaking great-grandmother. Her words slowed. "I should probably think about the kind of role models you and Dad were for us while I figure out what I'm going to do about Ryan." She opened the cabinet where I kept the tea.

"It's on the table."

"She likes tea? And she likes you. Two points in her favor. Plus she stood up for you. I like that too."

I hid a smile as I put the kettle back on. "I'm so glad you approve."

"Mom. I'm trying to be serious." She grabbed a mug and sat at the table, thankfully not where Eve had sat, and picked out a tea bag. "I'm sorry I just showed up. I'll make sure to text you first from now on." She bounced up from the chair and went to the pantry, snagging the cookies I always stocked, then back to her seat. "You know I'm going to tell Rissa, right?"

My girls had never been able to keep things from each other, something about which I was secretly grateful. I loved their close relationship and hoped they'd keep it forever. And if it meant they'd talk about me—which I expected every kid did about their parents—that was fine. "I figured as much. I'll call her too."

I brought over the kettle, then joined her at the table, snagging a cookie to go with my water. My hips would do better without the calories, but I needed to satisfy at least *one* craving tonight, so chocolate it was. We munched in silence for a few minutes.

Lila pointed her half-eaten cookie at me. "I have, like, a billion questions for you and none of them are ones I should ask my mother."

I laughed. "How about we give this a while to sink in before you ask them? It's really new, honey. There are things I can't tell you because I haven't worked them out yet." I decided to be completely honest with my adult daughter, who knew what it was to have an adult relationship. "And there are some things I don't want to share. They're between me and Eve, just like they were between me and Dad."

"I get that. I don't share everything with you, either."

I pretended to be aghast. "No."

My sweet, kind, wonderful daughter grinned. "And on that note, I'm going home. I might still want some advice about Ryan, but you're right. I have to figure out how I would feel, first." She finished the rest of her tea, then stood and hugged me again. "Love you, Mom. Sorry I interrupted."

"Love you too, honey."

When she left, I went back into the family room to grab my phone and turn off the television. As I passed by the sofa, I got a slight whiff of apples and cinnamon and smiled even though no one could see me.

I got myself ready for bed—brushed my teeth, washed my face, stared at the hickey on my neck that I'd have to cover up for work tomorrow—and climbed into bed. My mind kept running over the fact that Eve had known what the options were if we dated. She'd obviously thought about it, while I had been thinking I was alone in this attraction. What else hadn't I realized about her?

I wasn't quite ready to sleep, so I picked up my phone to see if Rissa had posted anything on social media about the engineering project she'd had to turn in today. It buzzed in my hand and I saw a message from that unknown number I'd seen earlier tonight. I opened it, and my heart fluttered.

Eve.

I'm sorry we didn't get to finish what we started but maybe it's for the best. There was a slight break in time between the two lines of text, as though maybe she'd been waiting for me to answer. *There's a jazz concert at the college on Wednesday night. Want to go?*

A date? That sounded . . . really nice, actually. I looked at the time she'd texted—just a few minutes ago—and texted back. *Yes.*

When my alarm went off the next morning, I groaned as I smacked it off. While I loved my job, Mondays were not my favorite days in the office. There was always a huge pile-up of email and voicemail, and it could only be worse after the festival yesterday.

I rolled over, and two things occurred to me at once. My boss had told me I could come in late today.

And I'd had almost-sex with that very same boss last night.

I pulled my pillow over my head and moaned into it. Maybe I could just stay here all day and pretend like she'd told me I could have the day off, and then we wouldn't have to have that awkward how-do-we-handle-this-in-the-office moment?

No, really, I couldn't. We were both adults, and I needed to do my part and act like one.

I was vain enough that I took extra care dressing. I wore a pair of slim black pants that Rissa and Lila had urged me to buy when we'd been shopping at our favorite thrift store because *they make your ass look incredible, Mom*. I'd laughed and caved, mostly because they'd been about five dollars. I'd figured they'd sit in my closet and I'd never have the opportunity to want to show off my incredible ass.

Hah. Score one for my girls.

I paired it with a tailored shirt that covered the hickey on my neck, some silver jewelry that matched the silver threads in my hair, and a little more makeup than I usually wore. At the door, I hesitated. Was it overkill? Like a teenager with her first crush, I went back to my room, stared at my closet, and waffled for about fifteen minutes.

Oh, screw it. *Nothing wrong with what you've got on, Talia.*

I got to the office later than I usually did and, surprisingly, the office was empty. Eve's computer was off, and no tea sat on her desk.

And then I remembered she'd said she had an early meeting. I booted my computer and pulled up her schedule. Right. Budget meeting, which meant she could be gone for hours.

I was both relieved and deflated, and how stupid was that?

Deciding my time would be better spent working and not woolgathering, I opened my email and winced. Fifty-three since Friday? Oy. I was going to need more coffee for this.

I went to the break room and filled up my *World's Okayest Mom* mug, then went back to my desk to start digging through the pile. An hour later, I'd responded to all of the ones for Community Relations, which left six. Two of those were about active investigations, which I forwarded as Eve had instructed me weeks ago. Three were about employment, which I sent on to HR. And one was an adorable thank-you note from Kiera, the little girl we'd met yesterday at the festival who wanted to be a fairy-princess-doctor-plishoffer-astronaut-dancer. Her parents had scanned the child's drawing and emailed it. Eve would want to respond personally to this.

Not a threatening one in the bunch, thank goodness. Maybe now that the festival was over, so was the issue?

I stood up at my desk and stretched my arms up over my head. My shirt rose up, and cool air brushed against my naked skin.

"G'morning, Tal."

I jerked my head up to see Eve standing just inside the door. Her voice was low and potent and, coupled with her eyes on the bare slice of stomach I *had* to be showing, it sent a shiver down my spine. I forced my voice to stay level as I tugged my shirt back down. "G'morning, Eve."

"Sleep well? Or were you too wound up?" The second the words were out of her mouth, she winced and mumbled under her breath. "Christ, woman. What did we talk about?"

I blinked. "Excuse me?"

She looked sheepish. "Reminding myself not to do this at work."

Her admission made me feel better about my own nerves. "Hah. I had that same conversation with my brain this morning."

She laughed wryly. "So glad I'm not the only one." She dropped her soft briefcase into her chair, started up her computer, then grabbed her mug and held it up. "Can I get you a refill?"

I picked up my own mug. "I'll go with you and fill you in on today's email."

"Sounds like a plan." As we walked I gave her the scoop, including the sweet note from Kiera.

Eve's smile was just as sweet. "I love those the best. They make up for the shittiest parts of the job."

I fixed myself another cup of coffee while Eve plopped a tea bag into steaming water. I stared, shocked. "What, no special blend?"

She scowled. "I'm out. Going to have to stop at the tea shop tonight."

Even as I made a mental note to see what she liked so I could have some at the house, I snorted. "You're as bad as any coffee addict, I swear."

Delia walked into the room. "Worse, even." Eve bared her teeth in a wolfish grin, and Delia laughed, then changed the topic to work. "No emails this morning?"

"Fifty-three of them, but none of them threatening," I answered, telling her the same thing I'd told Eve a few minutes earlier. "Though it looks like the event prompted some potential recruits to ask for more info."

"You passed those along to HR?" Eve asked.

I rolled my eyes. "Yes, ma'am. Just like you told me to do on day one."

She raised a brow, and heat sparked in her eyes. "Someone is a little testy this morning."

"Well, yeah. I'm not the only one, am I?" I asked in a sweet tone.

Delia laughed and turned the conversation again. "I heard we had a second arrest near the end of the festival. Anderson cuffed him when he took a swing at her, and he started spewing a bunch of garbage. Made some threats, but she chalked it up to him being a drunk who didn't like being told not to harass women."

Eve lifted a shoulder. "Shit like that happens." I tensed, and she sighed. "I told you, it's the nature of the job, Tal."

"I know that, Eve."

I flushed when Delia cleared her throat and looked back and forth between us. "Jeez, you two need to get a room."

I don't know which of us was more nonplussed, but I'd have to say Eve was. Fairly vibrating with tension, she started to speak—most likely to deny, which I understood in my head but twisted at my heart—only to be waved off by Delia.

"Your secret is safe with me. I think you'd be pretty great together." She lowered her voice, leaned closer. "You'd never—and I mean *never*—believe what happened between Colin and me when we worked together on that arson case year before last. If the chief knew, he'd kick my ass and take my badge. Trust me on that. But some things are worth breaking the rules for, y'know?"

I could tell it bothered Eve that a colleague believed she'd stepped over a firmly etched ethical line. It bothered me too, which was why I'd fought the attraction as long as I had. Not because of me, but because Eve was the very public face of this job and therefore had to maintain a sense of propriety. She loved what she did, she was good at it, and she was a career cop. I wouldn't do *anything* to jeopardize that for her.

When Eve didn't respond, Delia looked like she was sorry she'd opened her mouth, but I jumped in to soothe her concerns—and Eve's. "Nothing *to* hide. We're just giving each other grief." I forced a grin. "I've never worked for someone who had the same sense of humor as me. Sometimes we get a little off track."

Delia clearly didn't believe a word of it—*smart woman*—but nodded. "Understood."

With that bit of awkwardness between us all, we left the break room and headed back to our respective offices.

Eve was quiet for about fifteen minutes, but it wasn't a comfortable silence. Something was stewing in that brain of hers, that much was obvious. I kept darting glances at her over the top of my monitor, and then I couldn't take it anymore. "Eve?"

"Not now," she muttered. "You walking at lunch today?"

"Er, yes?"

"Okay. Then." She glanced down at her computer, back at me, and rubbed her temples. "Budget now."

I went back to the flier I was working on, but my stomach churned. Eve rarely if ever spoke in one-word bites, a fact I appreciated since I was a verbal person too. She generally fell into short answers if she was upset or angry, and I didn't like either of those options.

Time dragged but finally it was noon, and I changed from my work shoes into sneakers. I locked my computer, stood, and put on my jacket and, as though she'd been waiting for me to be done, Eve stood too and held out a hand toward the door. "Lead the way."

Chapter
EIGHT

fter I grabbed my yogurt and a piece of fruit, we left the building and turned right, heading downtown toward the walking path along the creek. I sometimes sat at a bench in the sun, so I went that way, only to find my usual spot taken. "Let's go there," I said, pointing to the amphitheater across the creek.

It was empty but for the two of us, and I sat, holding my silence. Eve had wanted to talk, so I waited for her to speak, but she just watched the people walking along the other side of the creek, ever alert. When the quiet stretched from one to two to four minutes, I opened my yogurt and started to eat.

"Did you know you lick your lip after every spoonful?"

I nearly dropped said utensil. "What?"

"You lick your lip. I noticed it right off. And now that I've kissed those lips, it's driving me crazy. I want you to take a taste of it, and then I want to taste you." My heart went all flippy-floppy—until she spoke again. "But this morning you told Delia there was nothing between us. Did you mean that?"

I'd known almost immediately that my denial had bothered Eve, but her words felt like shards of glass. "Do you think I meant it?"

Her gaze skittered away, and in that moment I wanted to take her in my arms. But we were in public, and she was in uniform, so that would probably be a bad idea.

"I don't know. This moved really fast, Tal. And I had a lot of time to think last night after I went home. I'm not—"

She didn't finish the statement, and the yogurt suddenly felt heavy and sour in my stomach. "I haven't played any kind of dating game for over twenty years. I'm used to the open honesty of a solid marriage, so I'm just going to say what's on my mind. I wasn't expecting this either—though I admit I wondered about it—and I was shocked when you came over last night. But you did come over, and we did start something. I don't want to end this before we know what could be, and I'm hoping you want the same, though I assumed you didn't want anyone else to know about it." I gathered my courage, my stomach turning over at the thought of what I was about to say. "But if you don't want to explore what's between us, if you want to go back to the way things were, then tell me now. Please."

She shook her head lightly, a small smile tipping up one side of her mouth. "You really don't pull any punches, do you? I want the same thing you want. But it bothered me when you told Delia there was nothing to hide." I went to explain, but she held up a hand. "You were protecting me. I get that . . . now. You're not the only one who hasn't dated in a long time. Not twenty years for me, but long enough. I got a little too caught up in my head."

Relief eased the knot in my gut. "I don't want this—us—to mess with your job, though."

She moved a bit closer, bumped shoulders with me. "And I don't want it to mess with yours, either. So we have to be circumspect, at least until we figure out what we've got. Agreed?"

"Agreed." I took another spoonful of yogurt, then deliberately licked my lips.

"Now you're just being mean," Eve said, her tone playfully pained.

I was rusty at this flirting thing, but hopefully it was like riding a bike and you never actually forgot how. I dipped my spoon into the cup again, but this time licked the yogurt off with my tongue. "Uh-huh."

Eve half laughed, half groaned. "I'm going to call you Tal the Tease from now on."

I giggled. Fifty-two years old, and I sounded like a damn teenager. But it truly *was* mean to torture her in public like that, so I changed the subject. "Do you think Delia and Colin really crossed a line while they were working together?"

She didn't answer for a moment, her eyes scanning the people walking by again. Did she ever get to turn it off, or was she always in cop mode?

"Maybe? Every time I've seen them, it's like standing next to a live wire, so I wouldn't doubt it." She turned to me and made a face. "But she's right about keeping things private."

"I know." I finished my yogurt, held out my apple. "You didn't eat. It's not much, but want this?"

Eve shook her head. "Not hungry yet. They had bagels at the budget meeting." Her eyes grew merry. "I might like a nice big bite of something similarly shaped later, though. Tonight?"

Just like that, I was aroused. But as much as I hated to—like, *really* hated to—I shook my head. "Can't tonight. I teach class for adults who are looking to convert to Judaism on Monday nights. We often run late."

Was it bad that the disappointment in Eve's eyes made me feel better?

She scrunched up her face. "If you're going to be like that, fine."

I had to laugh. "You're cute when you pout."

A shout from across the creek wiped the playful grin off her face in a second, and it went cop-hard as she zeroed in on two guys standing near a disheveled man in worn-out clothing. "So much for a lunch break."

When I moved to stand, she shook her head. "You stay here while I check it out."

Her job, I reminded myself. *Her job, and she's trained for situations like this.* I hid my worry for her as best as I could, and kept my voice mild. "Okay. But we're going to have to talk about your propensity for giving me orders."

"Nonnegotiable in this situation," she said as she punched a number on her phone. She held up a finger as someone answered. "Send patrol over to the foot bridge by the library. Two white males with a homeless guy. Might be nothing. Might be something."

She hung up and her attention stayed divided between them and me, until one of the young men grabbed at the guy's baseball cap.

"Oh, hell no." She took two steps, but looked back over her shoulder.

"Sit. Stay," I said, sketching a really bad salute. "Yes, ma'am."

She flashed that sexy grin, then turned and quickly made her way to the other side of the pedestrian bridge. It was amazing to watch the transformation from Eve the woman to Eve the cop. The woman was warm and relaxed and playful.

The cop was all business, with a hard edge that spoke of experience.

One of the troublemakers froze as she stalked toward them. The other took a belligerent stance, hip at an angle, his attitude cocky. They were both blond, early twenties, dressed like preppy frat boys, and they had privilege written all over them. I could only hear bits and pieces of what Eve was saying since her back was to me, but I heard nearly all of what the obnoxious one said since he was acting like an idiot, insulting her and arguing with her in a voice loud enough to carry over the narrow creek to the amphitheater. *Bitch cop* made me flinch, but Eve kept her cool.

I wanted to roll my eyes at his stupidity, but I was too busy trying not to panic as Eve stepped between them and the homeless man they'd been bothering. Because he was so unkempt, I couldn't tell if he was young or old or somewhere in between.

When the loud-mouthed frat boy whipped a hand toward Eve, things moved very, very fast.

Before I could even blink, she had him up against the wall, that arm twisted behind his back. His friend put his hands out low and wide in that universal *everything's good here, nothing to hide* gesture, and started talking earnestly.

As I watched, heart in my throat, a police cruiser pulled up, lights flashing, and another officer stepped out.

Eve released the guy against the wall and ordered him to sit on the ground, which he did with a sullen glare. The homeless man made hand gestures, and I realized he was deaf the same instant Eve did. She pointed at the man, then pointed at herself and then the steps. The man nodded, and they both walked over to the curved cement staircase as a second car pulled up, also with lights going.

We had a large deaf community, so I wasn't surprised to see that Eve knew some signs. It looked like she was rusty, but within minutes, the man nodded again. She stood and walked over to the newly arrived officer, talking with the woman for a few moments. Explaining the situation, I assumed.

And still, I sat.

At least my panic had eased off but, *damn*, my heart had nearly stopped when the guy had flung his hand out toward her.

Yet another officer arrived, and this one appeared to be fluent in ASL. He joined Eve for a quick conversation, before heading toward the homeless man still seated on the steps. Once everything was in play, Eve came back across the bridge.

"We can go back to the office now. Everyone is up to speed, and Detective Harris will interpret." She glanced over her shoulder, then back at me. "What?"

I just stared at her. "You're so calm, as if that guy didn't try to hit you or something."

Eve snorted. "Girl, that's nothing." The drawl faded from her voice. "I'm trained for this. And not to brag, but I'm good at it. He'll probably talk his way out of charges, but he knows not to mess around in my city again. I consider that a draw."

I wanted to argue, but I decided to take her word for it and move on. *Suck it up, Talia.* "Was the man he was bothering homeless? My synagogue runs a shelter out of our old downtown building, if he needs a place to stay. It's close to everything here and walkable." I pulled a piece of paper from my bag and wrote the info down, then gave it to her.

She took it and, as we passed the detective who was interpreting, she handed the note off to him.

We walked the rest of the way back in silence, like we had coming to the creek, but this time it was different. There was still tension between us, but not exactly about our relationship. A block from the station, as we waited for the traffic light to change, Eve turned to me. "You okay?"

Mostly? I was unsettled by what had just happened, at how easily a situation with a cop could escalate, but my brain would sort it out in its own time. "Yeah."

"Good."

The next two days seemed to crawl by, but then it was Wednesday night and I was waiting for Eve in the lobby of the college's auditorium before the concert. We'd driven separately because she'd been called into a last-minute late meeting and, since I'm a klutz, I'd managed to get printer toner all over myself and had needed to change. It had been easier to take two cars.

I looked around but didn't see her, then glanced at my phone. I was early, so we still had plenty of time.

I was just thinking it would be smart to use the bathroom before the concert started when I felt someone come up behind me.

"What's a sexy woman like you doing alone?"

The voice didn't sound familiar, but the refrain did. I stifled a sigh, pasted a pleasant look on my face, and turned, politeness engrained in me. It took a long few seconds for me to place him, but when I did, I had to stifle a groan.

His name was Jim ... something. He'd been a passing acquaintance of Seth's, not a friend. As a matter of fact, he had been one of the few people Seth had actively disliked. That in and of itself had been a red flag, because Seth had seen the good in almost everyone, but not this guy.

His eyes narrowed, and then a smarmy smile landed on his florid face. "You're Wasserman's wife. Well, his widow, I guess."

My stomach turned over at his absolute lack of tact. "He died several years ago, yes."

"I'm sure you miss having a man around to take care of you."

Oh, yuck. "Actually, we took care of each other. But yes, I miss him every day."

"There's some things a woman can't do for herself." Jim, whose last name I still couldn't remember and now *really* didn't want to remember, continued. "If you know what I mean."

The air stirred behind me and I smelled apples and cinnamon. Eve stopped by my side, her hand on the small of my back. "And there are some things only women can do for each other. Men not required," she said, her voice low and smoky with a hint of humor in it. She rubbed her knuckles against my cheek. "Sorry I'm late, babe."

Jim What's-his-name spluttered and backed away, his face a mixture of horror and fascination, and I burst out laughing.

"Saved by my favorite cop," I said softly, turning to face her. She'd changed clothes too, and was now wearing a long, flowy dress that flattered her toned curves. I'd only ever seen her in uniform, workout clothes, and, well, half-naked. "You look beautiful. Thanks for the bailout."

She grinned that devilish grin I loved so much, but then her mouth tightened. I glanced over to where she was looking and rolled my eyes. The asshole was furtively talking with another man of about the same make and model, and they both stared at us.

I smiled serenely and waved, then turned back to Eve. "Not sure how much of that you heard."

She grimaced. "Enough to realize he knew your husband. Should I apologize for interrupting and outing you?"

I snorted. "Seth was a great judge of character, and he had no fondness for Jim What's-his-name. I don't really care what he thinks. And if anyone has an issue with me dating a woman, they can bite me."

Another flash of that devilish smile. "That's what I'm hoping *I* get to do later tonight."

I flashed hot all over. "Eve!"

"I've been thinking about it since that damn apple, so it's your own fault." Her words made me laugh again, so loudly that people turned to look. Eve raised a brow. "Okay, it was funny, but not *that* funny."

"Eve was tempted by an apple." I wiped a tear, giggle-snorted. "I'm sorry. I can't help myself."

"You're the kind of person who likes corny jokes and puns, aren't you?" Eve asked, the amusement ripe in her voice. She put her hand on my back again. "Why don't we grab our seats?"

I shook my head. "Bathroom first. Because all that laughing, so . . . yeah." This time it was Eve who fought a laugh, but she followed me to the ladies' room. The door was open and the line spilled out into the hallway. "Ugh. Why is this always the case?" I grumbled.

"Because we have to sit," Eve said. "So unfair."

Several women chuckled, and the usual slew of joking complaints and suggestions followed.

We seemed to be the end of the line, and by the time I finished, Eve and I were the only ones in the L-shaped restroom. I washed my hands, and when I turned toward where she stood, she put her hands on my hips and pulled me close, kissing me senseless. "I've been wanting to do this all day long," she murmured against my lips. The door around the corner of the L creaked, and she stopped, squeezing my hips once before letting go.

As the older woman came around the corner, I spun back to the sink and washed my hands again, catching sight of myself in the mirror. My color was high, my cheeks red and my chest flushed. Eve stood behind me, a satisfied look on her face.

I tossed my paper towel in the bin and leaned close, murmuring in her ear. "And you say *I'm* bad. You're a dangerous woman."

"You'd better believe it," she whispered back.

We left the bathroom and headed to our seats, which were surprisingly good considering the late ticket buying. Of course, in the small auditorium, there weren't really any bad seats. There was a mix of people in the audience, college age and senior citizen, with a smattering of middle-aged people like Eve and me.

Eve was approached three times by older women in fancy hats, all asking about her parents and telling her about the new pastor. She was polite, but I could see her patience wearing thin. As the latest woman headed back to her own seat, Eve sighed. "Church ladies. When I talked to my mother last week, she told me the new pastor is a widower and her friends think he needs a wife. They're still trying to marry me off even though I'm a month shy of fifty."

"Do they not know—"

"Oh, they know I'm gay. I don't hide it. They just choose to ignore that fact." She swore under her breath as another woman began to approach. "My mother kept them from hounding me, but now that she and my father are in South Carolina, they've been pulling out all the stops. They all think they know a man who'll make me change my mind, and this month it's the preacher."

That had to be incredibly frustrating. "Want me to hold your hand?"

"Literally or metaphorically?"

I laughed. "Both?"

Before she could reply, the chime telling people to take their seats sounded, and this time her sigh was one of relief. "Saved by the bell."

"Amen."

I leafed through the program and realized I knew one of the performers. And unlike the Neanderthal out in the lobby, Seth had liked Darius Washington a lot, and his wife and I were friends, though it had been far too long since we'd gone out for lunch, something I needed to remedy. I pointed to his name in the program. "Darius is the head of the music department at the high school where Seth was principal. His wife, Regina, is one of my favorite people. She helped keep me sane after Seth died."

"Really? Darius and I went to high school together. Small world."

"It is. I haven't seen him play in a while. This'll be good. I'm glad you asked." I settled back happily into my seat, and we shared a smile.

It didn't take long for the house lights to go down, and when they did Eve's hand covered mine. I turned mine over and laced my fingers with hers, a sense of contentment filling me.

Our hands stayed linked as Eve swayed in her seat to the music. Her full-bodied enjoyment of it made me like it even more. I couldn't remember the last time I'd had so much fun at a concert.

And, as always, Darius was amazing. He'd made his mark with a renowned jazz ensemble and had toured for years, but had returned to his hometown to share his knowledge with others. The kids in his classes were incredibly lucky to have him for a teacher.

It ended far too soon, but when it was over, rather than leaving, Eve urged me forward to the stage. "We can say hello."

I felt a moment of weirdness but then pushed it off. "Sure."

When the theater was empty and the house lights went on, Darius came back out on stage to pack up his instruments.

"Nice job, baby," I heard from the front row. I hadn't seen Regina there, but I knew her voice.

I started over to her, Eve right behind me.

Chapter NINE

Darius's baritone was as deep and wonderful as I'd remembered. "Well, I'll be. How're you doing, Talia?"

"Good," I said as I reached his wife. I hugged her and smiled up at him. "You're still as amazing as I remember. And I owe you a lunch date," I said to Regina.

"Uh-huh, you do."

"Who's your friend?" Darius asked me.

Eve answered. "You don't remember me, do you?" She held her heart like it was breaking. "I'm the girl who saved your ass in Calculus by tutoring you every day during lunch for a month."

His eyes widened, a delighted grin creasing his light-brown face. "Get out. Eve Poe? And yes, ma'am, you did. I would've failed without you."

Regina smiled. "You knew him in high school? I didn't meet him until later. Maybe you should join us for girls' lunch so you can give me all the gossip about what kind of boy he was."

He groaned. "What'd I do to y'all?" All three of us laughed, and he looked down at Eve again. "I've seen you somewhere else recently, but damned if I can remember."

"Been in trouble with the law?" Eve asked, her face bland.

His eyes widened. "Uh, no. Why?"

She let him off the hook. "I'm with the city police department. Used to be a patrol officer, now I'm part of Community Relations."

I bumped her hip. "*Commander* of Community Relations, she means. And she won an award last month, so her picture was in the paper."

"Really. Has anyone asked you to speak at the high school for career day?" he asked, ever the charmer.

I bit back a snort. I knew how much Eve loved putting the spotlight on herself, which was not at all. "I'm Eve's admin. I'll check her calendar tomorrow," I said, earning an exasperated look from her. "Oh, come on. It's for kids."

Regina laughed. "Oh, girl, give it up. Talia's as relentless as humanly possible when it comes to the kids. I can't tell you how many times the rest of the faculty spouses and I wound up doing stuff for the school we never expected to. The new principal's husband doesn't know how to lay on the guilt."

"I wasn't *that* bad," I said, flushing.

Regina smiled. "I didn't say it was bad. It made us all family."

My heart twinged. "That came from Seth, really. You know how he felt about the kids in his care and the people who worked for him."

Darius hopped off the stage and joined his wife, slinging an arm around her shoulder. "This many years, and I still miss him," he said. "He was one in a million."

I hadn't expected this trip down memory lane, hadn't guarded myself against it, and my throat grew tight. It had been easy to dismiss the blowhard's insensitive comments in the hall, but Darius had been Seth's friend so his words meant something. "Yes, he was. He'll always be a part of my heart." Tears threatened, even though I was standing with a woman who'd made me think I might just possibly find the same kind of happiness again.

"Hell," Darius muttered, drawing me into a bear hug. "I didn't mean to upset you."

I squeezed him and stepped back, giving him a tremulous smile. "You didn't. And I'm doing fine, really. It's been four years, and I've moved on with my life."

Eyes still troubled, he pulled his wife close again, and this time, she spoke. "You're seeing someone?"

The last time we'd had lunch, she'd gently asked if I'd dated anyone since Seth. I'd told her no, so her question wasn't out of the blue. I shifted my eyes to Eve and took her hand, which she tightened around mine. "I am."

The couple seemed momentarily startled but then Regina grinned. "You're dating your *boss*? Haven't you always said fishing in the company pond is a bad idea?"

Relieved by her almost-immediate acceptance I had to laugh. "You sound exactly like Lila. She gave Eve grief when she found out."

"Girl's got a good head on her shoulders." Darius looked between us, and I could practically see the gears moving in his head as he tried reconciling the fact that I'd been married to a man but was dating a woman. "I guess you're happy, then I'm happy for you," he said, his voice still warm but slightly wary.

"Darius Washington." Regina frowned at him, hands on her hips. "Really?"

Surprise painted his features. "What? I said I was happy for them."

She turned to me and Eve and rolled her eyes. "Men. How about girls' lunch next week? The new Cuban place?"

"I'd love to." I hadn't talked with Regina since Rissa had gone back to school, and I was sure she had a million questions for me. "Eve?"

"Sounds good," Eve said, though I wasn't sure she meant it. Her voice was quieter than usual, and her eyes were guarded. My stomach twisted, but I didn't let go of her hand, and she didn't pull away. I squeezed once.

We said our goodbyes and headed out to the parking deck behind the building, walking in not-quite-comfortable silence. At this time of night on this part of campus, it was mostly empty, and I shivered.

Eve shook her head as though she'd been deep in thought and raised a brow. "Cold?"

"I hate parking decks. My mind always gets the better of me." Hoping to get her out of her mood, I rolled my eyes. "I'm expecting a serial killer to be lurking in the stairwell."

That made her laugh. "You watch too much TV." She patted the handbag over her shoulder. "Besides, I'd protect you."

"You're armed?" It was hard for me to keep my voice from turning up at the end. "Now?"

This time, she was the one who rolled her eyes. "Yes, always. I never know when I'll get pulled into something."

I mulled over her words for a moment. I didn't like it much—because carrying her weapon while off duty meant she'd use it if she had to, and the action would put her in the line of fire—but I'd have to accept it if we were together. The thought made my insides clench. "That's kind of scary."

She lifted a shoulder. "It's what my life is."

As it turned out, we were parked on the same level, the only two cars left. Hers was first, and I stopped with her. She stood there, staring into space for a long moment. I called her name but she didn't seem to notice. I was getting worried, so I touched her arm. "Are you okay?"

She started to nod, then blew out a sigh. "No, actually, I'm not. Though why I give a damn about what a guy I knew thirty years ago cares about my sexual orientation, I don't know." She paused. "No, I do know. It's because he liked and admired your husband, and I feel like he's judging me—and therefore you—which pisses me off."

My words came slowly, because I'd been thinking about that expression on his face myself. "I don't think Darius is the kind of guy to judge. Maybe he was just shocked and trying to sort it out in his head? I mean, he had no reason to assume I wasn't straight."

She made a rude noise and threw her hands up. "That shouldn't matter to him at all."

She was right, but I didn't have any response to that. This was all so new to me, and so far the few people who knew about me and Eve hadn't given me grief. I'd still been bisexual while I was with Seth—not that I'd been one hundred percent sure about it—but being married to a man, I hadn't had to deal with any bias. I didn't know how much shit she'd taken over the years for her sexuality, though I imagined it had been a lot.

I hated seeing Eve like this, and the need to touch her and soothe her was strong. I stepped close and put my arms around her. She squeezed me tightly and held on for a few long moments. When she broke away, she looked less stressed.

"It's getting late, but do you want to come over?" I asked, fiddling with the sleeve on her dress.

She pulled out her phone, checked the time, and winced. "I want to. I really do, but tomorrow I have part two of that budget meeting first thing in the morning."

"No problem," I said, stifling my disappointment. I must not have done a good job of it, though, because Eve's eyes softened and she grazed my cheek with her fingers.

"Liar. But it doesn't leave me nearly enough time to do what I want to do with you." She walked me over to my car, then turned me so I was leaning against it. She didn't touch me again after that, only braced her arms on the car on either side of my body. "If I put my hands on you, I'm not going to be able to make myself go home. One kiss. That's all I'll allow myself."

My heart leapt as she bent forward. "Then make it good."

Sixteen days. That's how many more days we had to wait to get some alone time. I thought I was going climb out of my skin, and Eve didn't seem to be doing much better. The budget meetings had consumed the rest of the week, so we'd planned for her to join Lila and me for Shabbat dinner Friday night. But then her mother had taken a bad fall and Eve had gone down to South Carolina to help out for a week or so. I'd handled the office with input from different officers they rotated in and out daily, and when Eve had come back to work the following Wednesday, she'd been nose to the computer trying to power through the things we hadn't been able to handle for her.

By midafternoon Friday, she looked like she was going to fall over. I put on my mom voice and told her she was done for the day, and she was coming home with me for a hot meal and a nap, not necessarily in that order.

She proved exactly how tired she was when she didn't argue, just followed me home and parked behind me.

I'd brought her to my room, kissed her, and told her to lie down, and by the time I'd gone to the bathroom and come back, she'd been out cold.

She was still sound asleep and I was in the kitchen, singing softly to the playlist on my phone. I was putting together the ingredients for an apple pie, and I had a chicken roasting in the oven along with potatoes and other root vegetables.

I'd made enough in case Lila showed up, though she probably wouldn't. She'd told me earlier this week she would make Shabbat dinner at her place, and she and Ryan would talk. She'd decided to allow Ryan to explain, and while it wasn't the decision I'd have made, she was a grown woman who had to make her own choices.

I had my doubts that Ryan would listen to what she had to say, really listen. My heart hurt for her, though I'd never expected them to last long-term anyway. He'd seemed selfish to me, and the cheating proved that. Plus, he'd never been all that comfortable with Lila's observation of her faith and the rituals that were part of her normal, regular family life. I didn't see her giving them up, because they were too important to her, and I hoped she made sure she told him that. It wouldn't be an easy discussion or an easy path if she decided to give him another chance, and my mother's heart hoped she'd give him the boot.

The phone rang and I picked it up, smiling as I saw the caller ID. "Hi, baby girl. Shabbat shalom."

"Shabbat shalom, Mom." Rissa sounded happy and relaxed, and I could hear people in the background. "I'm at Professor Levine's house for dinner. He's a new teacher this year, and he and his wife invite students every week. I came with a girl from my MechE lab. She comes every week, but this is the first time I've been. I hadn't realized how much I missed it. And guess what? He knew Dad. They were fraternity brothers. He said he met you once at a conference in New York."

I racked my brain, trying to remember. "David Levine? Tall, dark hair, deep Southern accent?"

I practically heard her grin. "Yep."

"I do remember him. We ran into him and then wound up having dinner. He seemed like a nice guy. I thought he was a high school principal."

"He was, but now he teaches here. Math department. He asked me to be a TA for his Calc classes in the spring, Mom. I'm going to do it. He's really funny, and he told me some stories about Dad that legit cracked me up."

My daughter could talk at the speed of light when she was excited, and it took me a few seconds to untangle the words. "That's great, sweetheart. Quite an honor."

She could also change gears at the drop of a hat. "Is your hickey-maker there with you?"

I burst out laughing. "Rissa Leah."

"Sorry, Mom," she sang, her teasing tone proving she wasn't repentant in the least. "But is she? I wanted to talk to her. It's not fair that Lila already got to meet her and I haven't."

Rissa and I had talked a bit last week about mine and Eve's relationship, but she was right. "She's sleeping. Her mother was in a bad accident so she's been away helping most of this week, and then she spent the last two days catching up at work. I made her take a na—" Before I could get the word out, I felt lips against the back of my neck.

"Something smells good in here," Eve murmured, sinking her teeth into the tendon between my neck and shoulder, making me shudder. Her arms came around my waist, her still-warm-from-sleep body pressing against mine "And while the chicken smells divine, that's not what I mean."

"Mom?"

Even though my daughter wasn't standing here, I turned eight shades of red. I stepped out of Eve's embrace and thrust the phone at her. "Rissa wants to talk with you."

Eve's eyes went wide, but she took the phone. "Hello?" I only heard a word here and there from Rissa's end, and Eve's first tentative and then amused responses as my daughter obviously grilled her. "Yes, ma'am," she ended, handing the phone back with laughter dancing in her eyes.

I put the phone to my ear. "You'd have best been polite."

Rissa's tinkling laugh came over the line. "I was. She sounds very nice, Mom. And I stalked her online. She's pretty and she looks badass in her uniform."

I grinned. "She not only looks badass, she *is* badass."

There was a commotion on the other end of the line, a female voice calling out for Rissa. "Mom, I have to go. I just wanted to call because being here tonight made me a little homesick, but I feel better now. I love you."

My sweet girl. "I love you too, baby. Enjoy your dinner. I can't wait to see you in a few weeks."

We hung up and I turned back to Eve, studying her. "You look about a thousand times better with some sleep. I'm not sure how you were functioning."

"Barely," she admitted, rolling her neck. "I probably should've taken an extra day off to decompress."

I put my hands on my hips and gave her the face that made my girls quake in their boots. "You think?"

She ignored my question and nicked a piece of apple off the cutting board. "Chicken and homemade apple pie? You're the wife I've always needed." She popped the apple in her mouth and bit down.

"I've gotten better at the cooking thing. Poor Seth had it rough when we first got married. I burned everything, and I had no idea how to keep a kosher kitchen. It horrified his mother, but mostly he just laughed." The memory was a good one, and I smiled. "You don't cook?"

She wiggled her hand in a so-so gesture. "I'm good at tacos and burgers and ribs and pizza—food teenagers like to eat. Derrick was a bottomless pit, and he *always* dragged his boys home with him. Now that he's gone, I'm doing more healthy cooking for myself. Baking is something I never got the hang of. But I don't love cooking. I do it because I like to eat."

"That's a lot. If it makes you feel better, I have no idea how to cook pork or shellfish, since I don't eat it."

Eve groaned. "No bacon or crab cakes? Ouch."

"You don't miss what you don't try," I said, making a pretense of looking over my shoulder. I lowered my voice. "Keep this to yourself, but . . . I allow myself one crab cake a year at the fair."

She chuckled. "Bad Talia."

"I know." I shook my head sadly. "If my girls only knew . . ."

She plucked another apple slice and popped it into her mouth.

I rapped her hand with my stirring spoon as she reached for a third. "Stop that. If you steal them all, we won't have pie."

"And that would be a tragedy." She glanced into the dining room, saw the set table. "That's a lot of work for just the two of us."

"It's not work for me. Not when it's Shabbat dinner."

"So like a big Sunday dinner for Christians?" When I nodded, Eve continued. "Ah. Mama cooks like a fiend for those. Says family is worth it."

Exactly how I felt. "I think I'd like your mother."

"She's one of a kind, that's for sure. I'm glad she's going to be okay. She scared the hell outta me." Eve went to the oven, popped the door, and bent over to peek in, sniffing appreciatively.

Since we weren't in the office and she already knew how I felt about her, I allowed myself to stare at her ass as much as I wanted to. All that exercise she did, all those morning runs—they really paid off. Since she'd come from the office, she was still in uniform. After her nap, it was rumpled, but the way the pants hugged her hips and butt and thighs—good lord. If she looked this good in clothes, I couldn't imagine how good she'd look out of them.

She turned and raised a brow as I lifted my gaze. "My eyes are up here?" she quipped, something I'd said to many a man who'd stared at my breasts instead of my face. I choked on a laugh. She cocked her head. "Tell me what you were thinking."

Oy, I was so very rusty at this flirting thing, but I'd give it my best shot. "I was thinking about how good your ass looks."

Her eyes dropped to the snug black pants I'd worn today, the ones my girls had made me buy. "I have those same thoughts about you, so I guess we're even."

"And what you'd look like out of those trousers." When she didn't answer, I swallowed hard. "Too much?"

She walked forward with purpose, stopping mere inches from where I stood. My heart thudded at the heat in her eyes and the way she locked her gaze with mine. She grabbed my wrists lightly, then played her fingers over the skin there and across my palms. I shuddered. Who knew hands were such an erogenous zone?

"Not too much," she said, her voice husky as she continued to run her hands up my arm, teasing the spaghetti straps of the cami I'd worn under a sweater. "I know this is all new to you, and I know we're moving fast. If you want me to slow down, I will. But we're not teenagers. I know what I like and what I want. I want you. Under me, over me, my mouth on you, yours on me. Like the first time, only more. So much more, and all night long."

My legs went so weak that if I hadn't been leaning against the counter, I'd have fallen down. "Mercy."

She grinned, and that was all the warning I got. Her head dipped and she took my mouth, not gently but with the pent-up frustration that I felt too after so many days apart. It was new and familiar at the same time, and it gave me the same adrenaline rush I remembered from those first passionate kisses I'd had with Seth and with the boys I'd dated before him. A rush born of newness, of anticipation, and it was wholly intoxicating. A moan slipped out, and she used the opportunity to dip her tongue into my mouth, brushing it against mine.

The spoon in my hand clattered against the counter, and she let out a throaty laugh. "How much longer until dinner?"

"An hour," I managed, though I wasn't sure how.

"That's a good start." She took my hand and started to lead me out of the room, but I tugged back.

"Pie."

"Damn it," she said petulantly. "I want that pie. Finish . . . fast. I'll help."

By *help*, she meant *not help at all*. Instead of working on the pie, she worked on me, brushing kisses on my shoulders, taking nips against my neck, slipping her hands under my cami and into the top of my pants, playing with my belly button ring.

My body went liquid hot and I rushed the rest of the pie, shoving it into the oven. I set the timer, then dusted my shaking hands off. When I looked up, Eve's eyes were molten amber and my throat went dry. My voice came out in a husky rasp. "Done."

Chapter TEN

"Thank God." Eve practically dragged me down the hall and into my bedroom. "Take those pants off." I dropped my hands to my waistband, but then she changed her tune. "No, wait. I want to undress you myself."

She drew my top off and nudged my bra strap down my arm.

"It has a front clasp," I offered, wanting her to hurry, hurry, hurry.

"I see that. But not . . . quite . . . yet." She licked a path along the top edge of my bra, teasing me with her tongue until I was squirming.

"Eve, *please*."

Another soft laugh, but she undid my bra and slid it off, freeing my aching breasts. My nipples contracted into tight points, and when she scraped her nails across them, I shuddered. "My turn," I demanded, but she shook her head.

"Not yet," she said again. She pulled me toward the bed and sat on the edge of it, then drew a finger from my sternum to my belly button, playing with my piercing again. "This is hella sexy. Is it sensitive?"

I moaned as she tugged at it. "What do you think?"

Her eyes twinkled with devilish intent. "I think I'm going to enjoy finding out just how much." She played a little longer, then undid the button on my trousers with trembling fingers.

I wasn't nervous, exactly, but it eased my mind to know she was as unsettled, and as desperate for touch as I was. Part of me, the part that believed I couldn't possibly be this lucky twice in a lifetime, was worried I was making too much out of these feelings I had that didn't want to be contained.

I ceased thinking and worrying as Eve drew my zipper down, kissing me just above the line of my panties. She shoved my trousers down my thighs. "Wonder Woman?" she said, a smile in her voice and on her face. "Love."

"They called to me," I said, resting my hands on her shoulders so I could step out of my trousers without falling over. "I have several pairs."

She set her teeth against my hip, nipping me there. "Sexy."

"I think so. You have this thing about biting," I said, almost mildly. "I like it."

"Good to know," She nipped at me again. "I like the little noise you make when I do it." All humor fled from her face as her eyes turned serious. "You sure, Tal? Really sure?"

I didn't even hesitate. "Really sure."

She hooked her thumbs in the sides of my panties, drawing them off, baring me to her. But rather than glancing down, she kept her eyes on my face, maybe waiting for signs of distress. I spread my legs the tiniest bit.

"Really, really, *really* sure." I was so ready for this next step, and if she stopped now, I wouldn't be held responsible for my actions. And since she was a cop, she'd probably have to arrest me. "If you don't do *something*, I'm going to strangle you."

She looked amused instead of threatened. "You can try. I'll enjoy taking you down." On that last word, she leaned forward and nuzzled my stomach—the one with the stretch marks and C-section scars—and then lower. "Mmm . . . coconut. I want to take a nice, long lick."

"So what's stopping you?"

Her eyes met mine, and then she stood so fast she'd have knocked me over if she hadn't grabbed my upper arms. She pushed me down onto my bed on my back with a laugh. "Not a damn thing."

I scooted back, grabbing a pillow to put behind my head so I could see Eve's face. She climbed onto the bed and nudged my legs apart, kneeling between them.

I could only see the top of her head when she bent down to keep her promise. Her normal, workday twist hung to one side and several spiral curls had escaped the confines of it. I'd never seen her this disheveled, not even after running. As she licked my stomach, she reached up with one hand to tangle her fingers with mine. She didn't rush right to the main event, but instead took her time, drawing out the foreplay, teasing me until I could barely keep still beneath her.

She shifted again, hooking one arm under my thigh, drawing my legs further apart. I felt the soft puff of air as she breathed against my bared, heated flesh, and thought I'd lose my mind. The noise I made was almost embarrassing and it made Eve laugh, but she squeezed my hand, then ran the tip of her tongue over my aching clit.

A shudder racked my body and my legs fell apart, and then her tongue was inside me, touching me in the most intimate of kisses.

My hips pushed up but she moved her arm and held me down with her forearms, licking and nipping and sipping like she'd never get another chance. When she added her fingers, my heart began to race as pressure built inside me. I was no novice to oral sex, but as good as it had been with Seth, it was amazing with Eve. She seemed to instinctively know what I'd like—maybe because she liked it too—and she used that understanding to her advantage. I bucked my hips again as she continued to eat me, and then all the heat coalesced and I went over, coming in a long, loud orgasm.

I lay there, boneless and sated, my chest heaving as she worked her way back up my body, coming to lie beside me on the bed, her head next to mine on the pillow, her hand splayed across my heart.

The sweetness of that made my throat tight, and I turned my head away, trying to hide the tears that escaped. Her hand touched my cheek and she leaned over me.

"What's wrong, Tal?" Worry filled her eyes and I hurried to reassure her.

"It's been so long since anyone has made me feel like this," I admitted. "But it's never felt exactly like this, either."

"Is that bad?"

I wiped the corner of my eye, then kissed her, tasting myself on her lips. "No. It's like . . . an emotional release on top of the physical one. And so different from the way my husband made me feel, but no less amazing."

The furrow between her brow eased and she rubbed a thumb over my cheek. "Good."

"Very, very good." I played with the buttons on her shirt, smiled. "But I'd like my turn now, and you have too many clothes on."

She groaned. "Jesus, I'm still in uniform. Don't *ever* let this get out. At least I removed my weapon first," she muttered under her breath, which made my grin morph into a flat-out laugh.

"Another secret? I'm going to have to start charging you to keep my silence."

"Extortion?" Eve sniffed haughtily, her brow raised. "I thought you were more honorable than that."

"Then my evil plan to snow you is working." I tugged her to sitting and drew off her polo shirt. She wore a sports bra that had no hooks, and since those torture devices required a contortionist's skills to remove, I didn't even try. "Take that off."

"Bossy thing, aren't you?"

"I have my moments. Off." Instead of waiting for her to finish, I went to work on her trousers, undoing the button and sliding down the zipper. She pulled up her bra, and at the same time, I drew down her pants. When I saw her underwear, I burst out laughing.

Eve lifted a shoulder. "What can I say? We both have good taste."

They were the exact same pair of Wonder Woman ones I was wearing. Rather, had been wearing, past tense, since she'd stripped them off me. "Or we both bought them on clearance because why not?"

"Or that." She dropped back onto her ass and shimmied the rest of the way out of her trousers until she lay before me in nothing but panties.

I quickly tugged them off. "On your belly." She gave me a *say what?* look, but did it, and I could barely hold back my groan. Her body was even better naked than it was in clothes, all lush curves and lithe muscles. I slicked my hands down her smooth back, over her toned ass and legs. "You're gorgeous, you know that? All that running gave you sleek muscles, but your curves are giving me really, really dirty ideas."

She laughed, low and hot. "Do your worst."

I continued to stroke her with the palms of my hands and then with my fingernails, raising goose bumps on her legs. With a deep sigh, she crossed her arms and rested her head on them. I bent down and nipped at her ass, then licked at the two small dimples in her lower back.

"Good lord, Tal." She gave a whole-body shudder as I licked her skin, tasting womanly sweat and apples and something that was uniquely Eve.

When I'd had my fill of her back—well, my first fill, because I definitely wanted to do this more than once—I guided her over so I could play with her front. Still naked myself, I straddled her, leaning down to take one taut peak into my mouth. This time, she was the one who made the needy noises, and they just inflamed me further.

For the next several minutes, I took my time exploring every inch of her—except the place between her legs. It was deliberate on my part, but I hadn't realized how it would come across to Eve.

She laid a hand on my head. "Tal, if you're not ready for this, I get it."

I looked up and blinked. "Ready for what?"

She sighed, shifted her legs. "You've touched me everywhere but—"

"A little worked up, are we? I'm getting there. Weren't you the one who said we could do this all night long?" I rubbed my nose against her stomach. "I'm never going to have a first time again, so I'm taking my time. Savoring it, you might say."

Her face stayed serious.

I cupped her cheek, kissed her soft lips. "I promise I'll tell you if something is too much, okay?"

Finally, she nodded. "Okay."

Then I went back to my work of torturing her—and myself. The tighter I wound her up, the more aroused I became. I shifted my body so I straddled just one of her legs and I drew a finger along the crease of her thigh on the other leg. "Open," I demanded, my voice deeper than normal.

"Bossy," she muttered again, but she did it.

The smell of her arousal was intoxicating. I hesitated the tiniest bit, not because I was unsure of my desire but because I'd never done this before. Then my visceral need for her overcame my brain's fear of doing something wrong. I brushed the back of my hand against the silky curls at the vee of her legs, then parted her with my fingers.

She was glistening wet, and instinct took over. I leaned forward and drew the flat of my tongue up her center. Her taste exploded on my senses, so different from what I'd been used to with a man, but So. Damn. Right. "You taste like heaven," I murmured, licking her again. "Does that feel good?"

"Jesus, yes." She lifted her hips as I pulled my mouth away for a second. "Don't stop."

"Now who's being bossy?" I tried a few different things, noting which ones made her squirm and which ones didn't seem to do much for her. She seemed to like it when I scraped my teeth against her tender flesh, so I did that again, this time slipping a finger inside her.

A keening moan burst from her throat. "Fuck, Tal. Fuck, you're good at this."

I *tsk*ed. "Language, babe," I chided, nipping her thigh. It really didn't bother me, but I loved riling Eve up. Her reactions got me every time.

"Girl, I am almost fifty years old. Don't even *think* I'm going to change my language for you." I giggled, and she reached up and pinched my nipple. "Smart-ass."

The sharp bite of pain went right to my core and my back bowed. With an evil grin, Eve pinched the other one and drew up her leg like she'd done during our first time together. We'd had the barrier of clothes that night, but now we were skin against skin. Her bare leg against my core made me whimper with need, even though I'd come earlier and Eve still hadn't.

Her throaty laugh curled around my heart and I grinned down at her. "You don't fight fair."

"Ever," she said smugly. "Remember that."

"Duly noted." As I rode her leg, I had to force myself to focus. I withdrew my finger from her, slipping it into my mouth and sucking on it. "Neither do I."

Her laugh was half groan and, while she was distracted, I tucked two fingers inside her and then three. She clenched around me, tight and hot, so I bent down, tonguing her clit. I didn't let up until she was gasping under my touch, shuddering through an explosive orgasm, her chest heaving.

Satisfaction flowed through me. My core still pulsed with need, but emotionally, I was content to lie beside her, stroking her until her breathing eased back to normal.

After several long moments, she turned on her side facing me and I did the same. "You okay?" she asked, tangling her legs with mine.

I'd lain like this with Seth so very many times—not in this bed, which I'd replaced when I'd repainted, but in this room—and it felt so good and so right that I felt the smile on my face as it bloomed. "I'm wonderful. You?"

"Mm-hmm," she admitted, playing with my breast, moving between it and my hip. "I'm thinking I'd like to do that again."

But then the kitchen timer went off, so I handed her a robe while I put on one of the men's XXXL flannel shirts I often wore around the house on weekends. Eve eyed it almost cautiously and I realized she might think it'd been Seth's, so I moved to reassure her. "I know, not exactly me, is it? But it's warm and comfy. I bought it at the end-of-season clearance this spring, and I wear it like a robe when I'm hanging out at home. My girls gave me grief but I noticed the other two I bought are missing, so I'm guessing one is away at college, and the other is in a tiny apartment in town." I shook my head in mock annoyance. "They think they're slick, but I've got their numbers."

"It looks good on you. Sexy." She started to unbutton it but the timer went off again. "Damn it."

I laughed and batted away her hand, rebuttoning the shirt. "Food first. There are things I still want to do to you, and you're going to need your strength."

She grinned. "I knew I liked you, Talia Wasserman. Lead on."

I woke the moment Eve slipped out of bed. One glance at the clock on my nightstand and I groaned. *Seriously?* "Where are you going? It's only six thirty."

"Shit. I was hoping you'd sleep in." She tugged her trousers on, searched for the rest of her clothes. "I have to run home, get changed, and head to the office."

I leaned up on my elbow and frowned. "On Saturday?"

She lifted a still-naked shoulder. "On Saturday. I missed a lot of days when I was in South Carolina and stuff needs to get done. I have a report due Monday, and with Thanksgiving coming up in just a couple of weeks, I can't afford to fall behind."

"I'll come with you and help."

She stiffened. "That's not a good idea."

I blinked and shoved up to sitting. "Why not?"

"It's your Sabbath. And besides, it wouldn't look right. Especially since we left together yesterday."

That was ridiculous. "We didn't leave together. We left at the same time, in two cars. There's a difference."

She wiggled into the sports bra. "Not enough of one for some people."

Ice slid along my spine. It wasn't always easy, but we kept our relationship completely platonic in the office. No innocent touches, no joking that might be taken the wrong way by anyone who happened to see us together. Even me prodding her to come have dinner last night had been couched as a mama-bear type of offer. "Did someone say something to you?"

She frowned. "No, but I don't want them to."

I got out of bed and pulled on the flannel shirt to cover the goose bumps on my skin. "If they do, so what?"

"We've talked about this." Eve's eyes narrowed, her voice tinged with frustration. "We have to be careful or things could blow up on us."

We *had* talked about it, and I knew she was right. Caution was called for, but I was really starting to resent having to hide our relationship just because she was my boss and I was her employee. It was like a thorn in my side, and I lashed out. "So, what? I'm a dirty little secret?"

Eve jerked back as if I'd struck her. "*What*? That's not fair."

It wasn't, and I regretted the hurtful words immediately. Work was work, with no room for anything personal. Period. I sighed. "I know it's not. I'm sorry."

"Yeah, me too," she muttered, her body stiff and unyielding as she finished dressing. "I've got to go."

"Eve, wait," I said, following her to the door. She flinched when I put my hand on her back, and I dropped it to my side, my stomach clenching. "I *am* sorry."

"I need to go."

And she was gone, taking my heart with her.

I did some chores and tried to relax, but all I could think about was the look on her face when I'd said the unspeakable. I wanted to call her, but I didn't want to disturb her at work, and wasn't sure she'd even answer if she knew it was me. It set off memories I wish I could forget, like arguing with Seth the night before he died, and I spent the entire morning unsettled and stressed out.

I was utterly relieved when she called me a few hours later.

This time, she was the one who apologized. "I shouldn't have walked out, but damn it, Tal. That *hurt*."

I'd felt like shit all day, and I felt like shit now. "I know, and I'm sorry. I shouldn't have said that. I'm just . . . I want to be able to do the things other dating couples do, you know?"

She sighed. "I feel the same way, but let's just see how this plays out, okay?"

"Okay." It was hard to agree to, but we hadn't been together that long, and I got why Eve wanted to be careful. If it didn't work out between us, and the world knew? Awkward, and potentially devastating for her career. "Will you come over later?"

"I can't tonight—boring family thing I won't subject you to." Her voice warmed slightly. "How do you feel about the Inner Harbor tomorrow?"

It was one of my favorite places in Maryland. "If we can go to the aquarium, then yes."

"I'll meet you at your house at nine?"

"Sounds good." I paused, not wanting to end the call. "Eve? I'm really sorry about what I said. It wasn't fair, and I didn't mean to hurt you."

"I know," she said softly. "I'll see you tomorrow."

I was awake by eight, dressed and ready for the day by eight forty-five. I'd had a restless night filled with dreams about Seth and the argument we'd had the night before he'd died. He'd been late coming home every night that week, working overtime, and my temper had gotten the better of me. He hadn't deserved it—just as Eve hadn't deserved me lashing out at her for something she couldn't control.

So when she rang the doorbell just before nine, I dragged her into the house, closed the door, and kissed her hard up against the closet door. I cupped her cheek, rubbed a thumb over it. "I'm so sorry. Forgive me?"

She slid her hand around my waist, leaned her forehead against mine. "Forgiven. I wish we could do what we wanted, I really do. It's not fair, but it's what we've got."

"I know." I sighed, then grabbed my purse from the table in the hallway, tugged a light coat off a hook on the wall. "Unfair sucks. That's all I'm saying."

She snorted. "No lie there."

After another—this time lingering—kiss, we stepped outside into the bright morning light and I squinted, putting on my sunglasses. "Who's driving?"

"You are. I don't trust you to keep your hands to yourself, so best to keep them occupied. Besides, I'm a better navigator than you are." She winked, then slid her own sunglasses on.

No lie there, either, but . . . "Hey. I'm not the only one who can't keep her hands to herself."

She laughed lightly. "Let's go before I change my mind and we wind up in bed."

"Wait, that's an option for today?" I asked, stopping in my tracks. I liked that idea. A lot.

"No. I promised my girlfriend we'd go on a real date to the aquarium, and I don't like breaking promises."

My pulse got all fluttery at her simply uttered but obviously heartfelt words. "Then let's go," I said, my voice husky.

I behaved in the car and so did Eve, and the drive was filled with running commentary on the bad drivers we passed. She had me sticking to the speed limit—mostly—and we found an all-day spot in a parking lot just a few blocks from the harbor.

The weather was beautiful for November, and I enjoyed the walk over to the National Aquarium with Eve, though I wished we could hold hands.

"We can't. We're still too close to home."

Oy, I said that out loud? "I know, I know."

I went quiet for a few minutes, silently stewing about it and trying to hide my frustration from Eve, but I'd never had a poker face.

She pulled me around the side of one of the buildings, out of sight of the tourists flooding the Inner Harbor, and stepped close but didn't touch me. "Tal."

I sighed. "I *know*, okay? I don't have to like it."

She blew out a breath. "You think this is easy for me? It's not. I hate it as much as you do. You have to give me some room here, babe."

"I'm sorry. Again." Guilt flooded me, but that was my baggage, not Eve's. Shoving it aside, I injected a teasing whine into my voice. "It's just . . . What am I supposed to do with all these *feelings*?"

Leaning close, Eve whispered in my ear. "Save them for the bedroom."

A shiver slid down my spine, and I laughed, though it was shaky. "Fair enough. But you'd better take your vitamins, woman, because I've got a *lot* of feelings I need to express."

"Counting on it."

We stepped back into the flow of people headed toward the aquarium, bought our tickets, then headed inside. I'd been here many times over the years on school field trips and family outings, and a plan hatched in my brain, but I kept it to myself as we started our tour.

"It's different being here without Derrick," Eve said. "He loved it when he was little. I think the scuba divers in the ground-level tank are what made him want to go to the Naval Academy. At one point he wanted to be a SEAL, but he changed his mind and decided to be a Marine like his father. He wound up getting his scuba certification, though. Tried to teach me, but I didn't like being that far underwater."

"Too claustrophobic?" I guessed.

"Oh, yeah."

We shared our observations and sat through a dolphin play session, then headed over to my favorite part of the aquarium, the multilevel tank that was mostly dark as you walked around it. I turned to Eve. "I have a very important question for you. Top to bottom or bottom to top?"

"Definitely top to bottom," she said. "It's the only way to do it."

I grinned. "Same for us. I don't understand the people who go the other direction."

"I knew I liked you."

"Same."

We wandered up to the rainforest, then started our walk down the ramp that wound around, taking our time and enjoying the sights. It was crowded, and dark, and without giving myself time to worry about whether or not it was a good idea, I reached for Eve's hand.

In the bluish light from the tanks, I saw Eve's eyes sparkle as she squeezed my hand and shook her head, a wry grin on her face. She leaned close, her lips tickling my ear. "Devious wench, aren't you?"

I smiled serenely at that, and we walked together, hand in hand, until we reached the end of the darkness.

I was loath to end our contact, but I squeezed her hand once and let it go, knowing it was the right thing to do. Hating it, but knowing it. We stepped out into the light again, blinking.

And came face-to-face with Rebeccah Kohler, a woman I knew from the synagogue, and her husband. I'd met him once, briefly, but he didn't attend services with her.

"Talia!"

"Hi, Becca," I said warmly, giving her a hug. I turned to Eve to introduce her to them and was surprised to see dismay in her eyes. It was only there for a brief moment, but I saw it.

"Kohler," Eve said with a nod.

I glanced at her. *She knew him?*

His smile was friendly though tired. "Lieutenant." He tugged Becca forward, looped an arm over her shoulder. "This is my wife, Becca. Bec, this is Lieutenant Poe. She's the commander of Community Relations." He cocked his head at me. "I'm Jeremy Kohler. I've met you before, haven't I?"

My mind raced. He was a cop? No wonder Eve had seemed dismayed. I nodded at him, smiled faintly. "At the synagogue a few months ago. I'm Talia Wasserman."

"That's right. Good to see you again." He smiled, then frowned. "Wait. Wasserman? I saw your name somewhere recently."

If I hadn't known Eve intimately, I'd have missed the hitch in her breath. I turned to her and watched her paste a teasing smile on her face. It didn't reach her eyes, but it would probably fool anyone who didn't know her like I did. "Well, at least I know you're reading your briefings on night shift," she said. "Talia's working in my office. She replaced Bev."

Understanding lit his eyes. "Now I remember. Sorry, ma'am. Night shift is a whole different world. I'm just coming back onto days after a three-month rotation on nights, and I'm still in zombie mode." He laughed, as did Becca. "Trying to get my days and nights switched back around is brutal."

We spoke for a few more minutes, and then the Kohlers headed out for the drive home, while we went in search of food.

Eve was quiet all through our meal, and I started to get worried, though I let her have the time to think. It wasn't until we were inside the car, away from anyone who might overhear, that she spoke. "And this is why we have to be careful. In town, and out of town. Because no matter where we go or what we do, there is always the chance we'll run into someone we know."

"He doesn't seem like the kind of person who'd care that we're dating." I slid a glance her way in time to see her *thunk* her head back against the headrest, eyes closed.

"He's one of the most solid officers I've ever met, and I'd trust him at my back anytime. But if he'd seen us holding hands . . ." She sighed. "I don't know. I just know that we can't risk it again."

My heart sank, but I had to trust her on this. This was *her* career on the line. "Okay. I hate it, but okay. We'll do this your way."

Chapter
ELEVEN

The day before Thanksgiving, I stood in my kitchen, sipping my first cup of coffee. I'd woken early, as if for work, but I'd taken the day off to get everything ready for tomorrow. Rissa was home, still crashed in bed. Eve was working so that she could have Friday off, since Derrick would be home on leave for the holiday. He was due to land at BWI tonight, and she'd asked me to go with her to pick him up. His fiancée was coming with him, and Eve was all twisted up about meeting her.

This Thanksgiving would be interesting, and the stress leading up to it was getting to both of us. We'd been bickering all week, pretty much about everything, but if nothing else, at least we'd come up with a solution for Thanksgiving.

Normally, the girls and I went to Noah and Rachel's house because theirs was the largest and Rachel's brothers all attended as well with their families. When I'd found out Derrick would be home, I'd asked Eve if she wanted to join us. But her family had a big Thanksgiving too, and if she went to my family's celebration, hers would be put out. Instead, we'd decided to do our own in the afternoon, at my house with my girls and Derrick and his fiancée. That way, neither of our extended families would feel slighted and our children could get used to us together before we shared that information with anyone else. We'd make the rounds to other people's houses later in the day.

I was a little nervous about the whole thing, though. I wanted Derrick to like me, to think that I was good enough for his mother. And while I was fairly sure they would, I needed my girls to like Eve. Rissa had only talked to her on the phone, so this would be their first meeting. At least Lila had come with us when Eve and I had spent the previous Sunday in DC exploring the recently opened National Museum of African American History and Culture, and that had gone well.

Over the last couple of weeks, it had become both harder and easier to keep things all business while we were at work. Easier, because we had the benefit of age and experience, and we spent the evenings together whenever possible. Harder, because the more time we spent together, the more we craved each other's touch. All those teens and twenty-somethings who thought women in their fifties were dried up and sexless had never met an actual woman in her fifties. I pretty much wanted her all the time, and the feeling was mutual.

The only person at work who seemed to notice our new intimacy was Delia, and it was obvious she'd told no one. Everyone else seemed oblivious to our personal relationship, and that made it easier.

It was our lives outside the office where I struggled. If we went out somewhere, which was rare, we didn't do it in our own backyard, going to Baltimore or DC instead. I still hated that we couldn't be open with everyone and live our lives as we wanted—movie dates, weekend breakfasts out, things other couples took for granted—but after running into Jeremy Kohler at the aquarium, Eve remained ultra-careful if we were anywhere we might see someone from work.

And though I understood the reasoning, and I'd agreed to go along with it, I resented it and I couldn't see an easy way out. I didn't want to give up my job with the police department because I loved it, but there was absolutely no way I would let Eve sacrifice her career for us. Yet, something was going to have to change before I lost my damn mind.

This worry about the damage that having our personal relationship discovered could do to our jobs vied with my nearly constant fear for Eve's safety. The investigation into the vague threats to female cops that we'd received before the festival had been stepped up, because whoever it was had escalated. One female officer had been out on foot patrol, and when she'd returned to her squad car, it had been spray-painted with the word *bitch*. A Maryland State Trooper had been lured to a burglary call and she'd been ambushed and knocked unconscious. Her car, too, had been spray-painted with the same word.

But no one knew who or why, and everyone was on edge.

I forcibly shoved the unease from my brain. Today was not the day for worry. Today, I had to prep for Thanksgiving dinner. I lifted my cup to my mouth again just as my phone rang.

"Talia." It was Eve, but her voice was tight, nothing like her usual, easygoing tone.

My heart raced. "What's wrong?"

She made a pained noise in the back of her throat. "I got a call from the chief a few minutes ago. You and I have a meeting on Monday with him. He's away for the holiday, or else we'd be in his office today."

My mind went blank, then filled with a million different thoughts at once "What? Why?"

"Someone saw us. I'm not sure who or where, but the cat's out of the bag and he was less than happy with me." She made another small pained sound, and my gut knotted as deep-seated fears resurfaced. Was she sorry we'd started this? But then she continued. "Goddamn it. I should've gone to him first."

"We'll deal with it. I'll resign if I have to. I can find another job, but you've worked too hard to lose your career because of me." I said the words instinctively as I tried to reassure Eve, and I meant them, but the thought of giving up this job that I loved made my stomach knot. While Seth's life insurance covered the mortgage, I still had living expenses and college tuition for Rissa and retirement to worry about. Never mind the fact that I was over fifty and the market wasn't exactly overflowing with job offers for women my age.

Eve made another noise, this one of annoyance. "We'll talk about this later, Tal."

Once again, I shoved my worries back into the recesses of my chaotic mind and slammed the door shut on them. There wasn't a damn thing we could do right now, and Monday would be here soon enough. "What time do you want me to pick you up?"

We were taking my SUV to the airport because it had more trunk space than the tiny car I called Eve's windup toy.

"Four, if you can. There's going to be a lot of traffic as people start traveling. Need to give ourselves some extra time." She sighed, and I could picture her rubbing the heel of her hand over her forehead. "I can't wait to see my boy, but I'm not sure about this woman. And now this, with the chief."

I wished I could hug her. "It'll all work out. You'll see."

After the longest drive to the airport I'd ever had and hoped never to experience again, Eve and I stood waiting for Derrick's flight to arrive. On the drive in, we'd discussed the meeting with the chief ad nauseam, and I was tired of thinking about it. I shut the worry down—something I was getting a lot of practice doing—and focused on the here and now. The baggage claim area was mostly clear, and we'd snagged a spot by the arrival board so she'd see Derrick right away.

She'd changed out of uniform into a pair of slim jeans tucked into flat leather boots and a soft sweater that kept slipping to the side, baring one smooth and sexy shoulder. With her phone in her hand, she began pacing, muttering under her breath. I watched her, both amused at her uncharacteristic behavior and wanting to yank her out of her weird head space.

When she passed by me on her fifth lap around the still mostly empty area, I reached out and snagged her by her belt loop, pulling her to a stop. I got close behind her and whispered in her ear, sliding my hand around her waist and just under that delicious sweater. "You're going to wear a hole in the carpet, babe."

She sagged against me the tiniest bit, but steeled her spine almost immediately. "Can't help it. Have to move."

I kissed that bare shoulder lightly, ignoring the side-eye I got from a sour-looking woman standing nearby, then released my grip, letting her pace.

If it helped, it helped.

Within the next twenty minutes, the luggage area became a sea of people. I saw a large group of young men and women in fatigues walking toward us, and then Eve let out a small, stifled sob and was running, flat-out running, toward a tall young man with a mostly shaved head and a grin that was exactly the same as hers. I'd seen pictures of Derrick, but they didn't do the family resemblance justice. He dropped the bag he carried and scooped her up in his muscled arms, squeezing the hell out of her.

My eyes teared up and my throat grew tight.

Eve kept touching him as though she didn't believe he was really there. I hung back, not wanting to intrude on this emotional moment, and I noticed a petite, dark-haired, olive-skinned young woman doing the same, her eyes also suspiciously bright.

It didn't take a genius to figure out this was Derrick's fiancée, Gabriela Munoz. She didn't rush over, didn't insist on being part of this mother-and-son reunion, and I liked her immediately for that.

I walked toward her and quietly introduced myself.

Travelers flowed around the island that was Eve and Derrick, though several people stopped and thanked him for his service. I realized this same scene was going on all around us, and in a big way.

Something must've shown on my face because Gabriela spoke up, her voice thick. "The flight was about one-third service members. Various branches and from different duty stations, but we all came through Germany. Everyone was so nice. This is . . ." Her eyes flowed over. "Amazing."

It really was.

We weren't in any hurry to get home, so I did some people watching while Eve reassured herself her son was in one piece. People were starting to grab bags off the carousel, and Gabriela and I moved over toward it. "Derrick's looks like everyone else's."

I realized what she meant as a whole stream of green bags exited from between the fringed black rubber that separated the airport's side of the luggage area from the patron side. "Oh, boy."

Gabriela laughed. "His will have his last name stenciled on it." She snagged a desert camouflage bag from the belt. "This one is mine. Was Papa's from when he served." She was a tiny thing, but she hefted it with no problems, dropping it behind her.

We watched the bags go 'round and I read the names. *Ortiz, Anderson, Connelly, Luciano, Ahmed, Wisnewski, Wong, Stein, Kawahara, Davis.* The stream continued, and finally I spotted Derrick's bag emblazoned with *Poe.* "There it is."

Before I could grab it, a muscular arm reached around me and lifted it like it weighed nothing. "I've got it, ma'am."

Eve was right there beside her son, her face as content as I'd ever seen it. She held her hand out to me. I took it, and she drew me close to her side. "Derrick, this is Talia. Tal, this is my baby."

He laughed in a deep baritone as he rolled his eyes. "Mama. Haven't been a baby in a long time."

She patted his cheek. "You'll always be my baby."

He smirked but inclined his head in acknowledgment. "Nice to meet you, Talia." He pulled Gabriela close, nuzzled her temple. "And this is Gabriela Munoz. Gabri, my mother, Eve Poe."

Eve studied Gabriela with what I always called her cop face. Slightly suspicious, ready to detect bullshit in a single word. I'd seen her use it on recruits who helped us with Community Relations events and it was quite an effective method of intimidation. I stifled a sigh.

Gabriela shifted slightly on her feet, moving closer to Derrick.

Finally, Eve nodded. "Gabriela."

I slid a glance Eve's way and mentally shook my head. I knew how hard it was to let your kids fall in love and risk heartache, but she was going to have to ease back a little. I'd work on her, because from what I could see, Derrick and Gabriela looked like a lovely couple.

We made our way out of the airport and to my SUV, and then we went home, which took nearly as long as the drive to the airport had taken.

Exhausted, I dropped Eve, Derrick, and Gabriela at Eve's duplex. When Derrick and Gabriela went inside, I held Eve back. "Go easy on them, babe."

She wrinkled her nose. "I'm gonna make that girl sleep on the sofa."

"Eve," I chided. "Really?"

She sighed. "No, not really, but I should."

I rolled my eyes. "So if you stay over while Rissa's home, you should sleep on the sofa?"

"There you go being all logical," she muttered. "No."

I had to laugh at her petulance. "Go enjoy time with your son. I talked a bit with Gabriela while you were with Derrick. She's a nice person. I think you'll like her." I slid my hand on her waist, pulled her so we were pressed close. I kissed her once, lightly, but then I deepened it. "I'll see you tomorrow."

She kissed me back, then leaned her forehead against mine. "Don't kill the girl. Got it."

I laughed again and went back to my car, already missing her presence as I drove away.

When I got home it was to discover that Rissa had made a pumpkin pie for tomorrow, and was in the process of making a kosher apple cake, one of our family's favorite recipes. I kissed my daughter's forehead. "Thank you, sweetheart."

Her brown eyes shone bright. "Did Eve's son get in okay? I thought everyone would come here."

"He did. I just dropped them all off at Eve's house, but they'll be here tomorrow." I shuffled things around in the fridge, organizing them for easy prep in the morning. "They were really tired."

I dropped onto a stool at the counter and watched Rissa move competently around the kitchen. She favored her father's side of the family, and while both girls had the Wasserman nose, that was where their physical resemblance ended. Rissa was tall, easily five nine, and slender where Lila was curvy. Her hair was brown and curly, though when she'd left for college at the end of the summer it had been long, and now it was super short and cute. I'd been taken aback when I'd first seen the drastic change, but now I liked it. It fit her.

"Mom, can I ask you something?"

"Anything, you know that." Tired as I was, I relished the chance to sit and talk with my daughter—I missed her when she was away at school. I inclined my head. "What's up?"

Rissa shifted from foot to foot. "How did you know you liked Eve? Like, as more than friends? What was it that made you think you were interested in her?"

"I just knew," I said, but that was a pretty nonspecific answer. "I'm not sure I know how to describe it, but things felt . . . right. Flutters in my stomach. Wanting to spend time with her. She makes me happy, like Dad did."

Rissa shook her head and bit her lip. "I get that part. I meant . . . what made you realize you liked *women*?"

I blinked, and regarded my daughter closely. New haircut. Different clothes. No mention of male friends, or dating any guys. A lot of talk about Jules from MechE lab. "Honey, are you telling me you're gay?"

She gave me a sidelong look. "Maybe?"

I stood and pulled her into my arms for a hug. "You know I'm fine with that, right?"

She snorted as though she was questioning my sanity. "I know *that*. But that's not what I'm asking. I really mean maybe. How do you *know*?"

Aha. My scientific, studious daughter hadn't dated in high school, hadn't talked about crushes, and in fact had told me she had no interest in dating. She'd had a group of close friends, boys and girls both, and none of them had dated either. When she hadn't told me about anyone during her freshman year of college, I'd assumed she just hadn't met anyone who measured up, and I'd been fine with that. I'd wanted her to get her life settled first, anyway, and she'd been so very young—only seventeen when she'd gone off to college. But maybe there had been more to it.

"Well, for me, it was more a case of accepting that I liked women as well as men." I shared more about my own experiences with her than I had with her sister, because I understood how vitally important this conversation was. "When I was young, maybe early teens, I realized I was looking at girls the same way I was looking at boys, but I never did anything about it. Times were different then, though. Being gay or lesbian wasn't easily accepted, and I don't think I ever knew anyone who was bisexual."

I squeezed her again, then sat back down while she went back to work on the cake. She'd always been like this, happier to talk while she was focused on doing something else.

"But then I met Dad, and I loved him, so it didn't really matter, you know? And after he died, I didn't think about anyone for a long time, because I was still grieving. When I met Eve, I felt that attraction again, very similar to how it had felt with your father. I guess what I'm saying is I just *knew*. But knowing is one thing. Accepting it is another."

"I feel that way about Jules. She's the girl I was telling you about, my partner in my MechE lab. I get all tongue-tied around her." She looked at me, her eyes troubled. "I tried dating some guys last year. They were nice, and the kissing was okay, I guess, but their kisses didn't make me feel the way I do even just talking with Jules."

My heart ached for my baby's confusion. "Honey, you're not required to like guys, honest. I know the world tries to make women believe they have to, but I want you to be happy, and kissing should be far more than just okay. If you find a woman who makes you happy, then I say go for it. I guess my question is, does Jules feel the same way?"

Rissa lifted an elegant shoulder. "I don't know. Maybe? I think so."

"Then you owe it to each other to find out," I said. "Start with a conversation and see where it goes from there."

She nodded, and we left it at that.

Thanksgiving morning dawned cool and crisp, the sky a deep, pretty blue with puffy white clouds. I'd gotten up early to put the turkey in the oven, and now I was getting other things ready.

Eve had already texted me this morning to tell me *That girl made herself right at home in my kitchen.*

I'd laughed, and sent back a text. *That's good, since you don't like to cook.*

I was still grinning when another text came in. *Whose side are you on, anyway?*

I took a moment to compose my reply. *Always yours. Your side, your back, your front . . .*

Then my phone rang.

"She made me breakfast, Tal."

Eve sounded put out, and I laughed. "And this is a problem, how?"

A gusty sigh. "She's making me like her, damn it."

"And no woman will ever be good enough for your baby boy." I *tsk*ed. "If he's going to get married, isn't it better for him to be with a woman you actually like?"

"There you go being all reasonable again. Remind me why I put up with you?"

"Because I give you lots of screaming orgasms?"

"Mom!" Lila's horrified voice came from behind me. I hadn't even heard her come in the door. I turned just in time to see her put her hands over her ears, red splotches on her cheeks and her eyes shocked. "Ew. I love Eve, but I did *not* need to know that."

Eve spluttered hysterically on the other end of the line, and her words were full of laughter. "You go deal with your kid. I'll go deal with mine. We'll see you around noon."

I hung up the phone and regarded my daughter. "Weren't you the one who said you knew I had sex?"

"*Stop.* Forget I ever said it," Lila pleaded, her hand out as if to ward off something evil. She covered her ears. "La la la la la la la not listening."

I laughed, then pulled her hands off her ears. "Your sister is upstairs in bed watching the parade. She said to send you up when you got here." I hoped Rissa would want to talk with Lila about what she'd told me last night, but I wasn't sure. I handed her a box of donuts, our annual Thanksgiving breakfast tradition. None of us wanted to fill up on real food before it was time for the feast. "Don't eat all of them."

Lila kissed me on the cheek and bounded upstairs. When they'd been young teens, we'd converted the angle-ceilinged second floor, which had been a dark and dreary attic space, into two cheerful, light-strewn bedrooms with a small shared bathroom. Rissa's room was still her room and would stay that way until she was done with college, but when Lila had gotten her own place and taken her furniture, her room had become my craft room.

Upstairs, boards creaked and something crashed to the floor, and I figured Lila had jumped on the bed. I went to the door and yelled up. "Girls!"

A chorus of giggles ensued, and it did my heart good. Though they might be young women now, they were still my little girls.

It took me about an hour to finish prepping my side dishes, including my special homemade stuffing which I put in a slow cooker instead of the bird. I tasted it and sighed. I hadn't been raised in a kosher home and, though I'd kept one for over twenty years, sometimes I really missed bacon in my stuffing. This year was, apparently, one of those years.

When everything was cooking or ready to be heated up, I went to my room to grab a shower. I closed my door, then stripped, and as I headed for the bathroom, my phone buzzed.

Chapter
TWELVE

I t was Eve, and warmth suffused my heart. "Hey, babe. What's up?" I asked.

She made a rude noise. "They're having sex in my house."

I laughed. "He's a grown man. And they're getting married."

"Would you want Lila and her boyfriend to be messin' around under your roof? Be honest."

I winced. "Point taken. And anyway, pretty sure they're over for good. She didn't say she invited him to dinner."

"Mm-hmm. And what if she had? I know you didn't like him, but who was it who said you're going to have to let things happen? Let me think . . ."

"Now that was just mean. And on a holiday too. See if I give you pie later."

There was a beat of silence. "I'll take some cream pie."

The laugh that burst from me sounded like a snort. "It's like you're twelve."

"Takes one to know one." I heard the smile in Eve's voice. "What are you doing right now? I'm trying to stay on the other side of the house."

The devil stood on my bare shoulder and whispered in my ear. "Getting a shower. I'm naked and I'm going to get very, very wet."

"*Girl.*" That one word held so much feeling that it was almost as if she was standing beside me. "You are killing me."

"I'd much rather . . . do other things to you." I'd almost said *make love to*, but I'd been very careful not to use the L word. I knew what I felt for Eve was likely love, but it was still so new that I didn't want to jinx anything. And I think she felt the same about me.

Maybe.

"Like what?"

"Are we really going to have shower sex by phone?" I countered. "Why don't you leave the directions to my house for Gabriela and Derrick? That way we can have real live shower sex."

A huff of air. "With your girls in the house?"

I gave a half laugh. "Goodness, I actually forgot. I've gotten so used to having you here, alone. So maybe not. Not today, anyway."

"Phone sex it is." I heard a rustling noise and imagined Eve in her lush bed. It was a hedonist's dream, with soft sheets and fluffy pillows and a thick comforter. One of the best days I'd spent in recent memory had been a Sunday morning in that bed with Eve, watching a marathon of our shared favorite show, and having long, slow, incredibly intense sex.

Since my phone wasn't waterproof, the shower was out. I made beeline to my door to lock it, then climbed back into bed, still naked. My hand drifted between my legs. "I'm touching myself, babe. Now you do it. I wish you were here with me." I closed my eyes, imagined the scene. "I want you over me, your mouth on me while I do the same to you. I want those to be my fingers inside you, teasing you until you can't take it anymore."

A soft moan from Eve. "Oh, God. It feels good but not as good as when you touch me. Get the green monster out."

I laughed and groaned at the same time. The green monster was this long, incredibly thick veined dildo that Eve had brought over one night. And yeah, it was a garish green. She'd said she'd liked it better than any of the supposedly flesh-colored ones, but I'd just stared at it in shock and maybe a little bit of horror. It was slightly curved with a bulbous tip, and I'd been hesitant, though Eve had convinced me to give it a try. I'd agreed, and when she'd used it on me and it had hit a certain spot, I'd completely lost control.

Whenever she was in a feisty mood, she pulled it out and tortured me with it.

I opened the drawer and snagged it out. I could barely wrap my fingers around it, and I'd never imagined something this big would fit inside me or that I'd enjoy it, but both things were true. "Got it."

"Run it between your folds like I do, but don't put it inside yet."

I rubbed it through the slick wetness between my thighs, my breath becoming unsteady. "I bet you only have one finger inside you. Slip another one in there and if that's too easy, put a third in, then slide them back and forth."

Her laugh was ragged. "Done." She must've moved, held the phone low, because suddenly I could hear the lush, wet sounds as she moved her fingers in and out. "That feels so good. Now put that monster inside you, but no fucking yourself with it. Not yet."

Knowing she was aroused made me even wetter, and though I'd never tried it this way before, I knelt on the bed facing the headboard, then sat on the head of the dildo until it was just inside me. I bit my lip. There was always a stretch when it went in, a burn that was so damn good I wished I could prolong the feeling. I gasped as the ridges passed over my swollen flesh, and the temptation to move up and down on it was so damn tempting. "Oh, I want to." I sank onto it a bit further, spreading my knees out as it slid deeper inside me. "I'm sitting on it right now," I panted. "I need to move."

"Sitting on it? Jesus. Next time we're alone you're showing me that." Her voice hitched, became breathier. "Four fingers, just for you."

Stars exploded behind my eyelids. "Make yourself come, babe. Now."

Her voice hitched again. "You . . . too."

I sank as low as I could onto the dildo, then slicked my wet finger over my clit. It didn't take long until I was spasming around the thing, my head thrown back and the muscles in my neck taut as I tried not to shout. "Oh, Eve."

"Talia," she cried out, then made that familiar, deep noise I knew and loved, the one that told me she'd flown over the edge. "Want you."

We lay there, each in our own beds, silent for several long minutes as we came back down to earth. When I could speak again, I kept my voice low. "That was . . . wow."

Eve laughed softly. "Yeah."

We talked for a bit, the same kind of pillow talk we shared in bed together. It was better in person, when I could touch her and be touched by her, when we shared small strokes of fingers and hands, lazy kisses and quiet intimacy.

"I should probably go. I need that shower now more than ever. And I still have a few things to get ready." A shadow crossed my mind, and I spoke before thinking, the words spilling out. "I'm worried about Monday."

Eve's sigh was deep. "So am I, but we'll get through it. Let's just forget about it for today, okay? Enjoy this time with our kids."

It was a good plan, but it was easier said than done. It hadn't been out of my mind for a single minute since she'd told me about it. "Yeah."

We hung up and I took a fast shower, though my legs were still a little unsteady. I smiled to myself as I dressed, putting on the new bra and matching panties I'd bought to tease Eve, and then colorful tights and a long, filmy shirt over them. No real waistband to worry about, plenty of room for food. Perfect.

I did my hair and makeup quickly, then headed back to the kitchen. Everything smelled divine, and I couldn't help but snitch a bite of the crispy part of the stuffing.

As though the girls had heard me finish in the shower, they both came downstairs, carrying an almost empty donut box. "Girls," I chided.

"What? We were hungry," Rissa said, an impish smile on her face. "Besides, I'm on break and there are no good donuts around campus."

"She ate most of them," Lila said, ratting on her sister in a singsong voice. "I was the good child."

I laughed. "You're both good children . . . most of the time. Now help me set the table, please." I raised a brow at Lila. "No Ryan today?"

"No Ryan, ever." Lila's face darkened and, as Rissa squeezed her hand, she squared her shoulders. "So, how many of us?"

My daughter was a strong young woman, and while the decision was hers and I'd never have made it for her, I was glad she'd kicked him to the curb. I studied my table with a critical eye. "The three of us, and then Eve, Derrick, and Gabriela. I think we can get away without putting in the table leaf. It'll be a little tight, but we'll have an easier time moving around it."

Rissa cocked her head. "We could go buffet style if you want. It'll make more room on the table."

I eyed the breakfast bar. "Good point. Let's do it."

The girls set the table and I pulled down serving platters. There was a lot of idle chatter until Rissa spoke up. "I can't wait to meet Eve in person."

My stomach fluttered with apprehension, but then Lila added her two cents. "She's pretty cool. Just put in your earbuds when she and Mom get mushy, or you'll hear things you do *not* want to hear."

"You mean like when we heard her and Dad?" Rissa shuddered, though her eyes held a grin.

Lila laughed. "Exactly like that."

I groaned and shook my head. "Did I say you were nice girls? I lied." This dissolved my daughters into fits of laughter, and it took everything I had to maintain the façade of my mock annoyance. "None of my special stuffing for either of you."

More giggles.

That set the tone for the rest of the morning as we prepared for our guests. There was much laughter and joking, which made my heart happy. And I enjoyed listening to my daughters catch up with each other. They'd always been close, but when Rissa and Lila teased each other and talked about their respective lives, I was glad to see it. As I'd thought many times since Seth's unexpected death, at least I knew that if anything happened to me, my girls would have each other's backs.

I pushed the thought away, checked on my turkey, then jumped when the doorbell rang. I darted a glance at the clock—not quite eleven thirty, so it was too early to be Eve and family.

"I'll get it," the girls both said, and they raced to the door practically tripping over each other.

I continued doing what I was doing, and when they came back, Rissa was leading the way while Lila carried a gorgeous fall flower arrangement. "What on earth?"

"There's a card," Lila said, placing the flowers in the center of the table.

"Oh, Eve," I murmured under my breath as I grabbed the card. I'd *told* her she didn't need to bring or do anything, that we had everything covered and she should put her whole focus on Derrick. But I was wrong—they weren't from her. "They're from Gabriela and Derrick. That is so sweet."

The girls and I finished making and set out the appetizers. For the last thing to do, I turned the matzoh ball soup on to simmer, just as the doorbell rang again.

The girls raced to the door. Again. I grinned and followed, laughing as they jockeyed over who got to answer it.

Rissa won.

She opened the door with a wide smile. "Hi there! I'm Rissa. Happy Thanksgiving. Come in so we can start noshing." She grinned, stepped back. "Mom wouldn't let us eat anything until you got here."

Eve laughed and held out a hand. "Good to meet you, Rissa. Your mom talks about you all the time." She smiled at Lila too. "Both of you, really."

Rissa ignored her hand and tackle-hugged her instead. "You're prettier in person than on the police department website. And Mom talks about you too."

Eve squeezed Rissa back, then let go. "This is my son, Derrick, and his . . . this is Gabriela." I lifted a brow, but before I could say anything, she revised her comment. "Derrick's fiancée."

Handshakes and hugs all around, and then Derrick, Gabriela, Rissa, and Lila went off into the kitchen, leaving us alone in the hallway.

"That wasn't so bad, was it?" I murmured, pulling her down the hallway for a quick moment of privacy.

"I saw your face. You got your point across," she muttered, scowling. "It's a good thing I like you."

"I like you too." I fingered one of the soft curls that framed her face. "So pretty when you wear your hair down and natural." I let go of that and traced her cheek, then the side of her neck until my fingers rested against her chest, fiddling with the necklace she wore. "Also pretty. This is the one you bought at the art festival, isn't it?"

Her voice was thick. "Yes. And if you keep touching me like that, we'll wind up in the bedroom and our kids can fend for themselves."

My body quickened. "I'd be fine with that."

Her eyes heated. "You are a bad, *bad* influence, Talia. And if it all didn't smell so damn good, and if the kids weren't here? Dinner would wait."

Since we'd wound up in bed with dinner burned several times, I knew it wasn't an idle threat. "Eve is easily tempted, eh?"

She let out a half laugh and then spun me so my back was against the wall. "So easily." She fiddled with the buttons on my shirt and made like she was going to undo one. "What do you have on under this?"

I smiled smugly. "Nothing but a bra. A new one, just for you."

She groaned. She knew my propensity for lacy bras and panties, and she liked me in them . . . and liked divesting me of them. "They'll save us leftovers, right?"

I kissed her on her nose. "Doubtful. Let's go be sociable and grab some goodies."

"So you know, I'm agreeing because my baby's only here a few days. Otherwise your goodies would be naked and under me in thirty seconds."

"Augh!" Lila's voice floated down the hall toward us. "I was going to tell you we were starting to eat, but . . . gah. Don't you two *ever* stop?" She spun around and stomped back to the kitchen, and we heard her rat us out to the others.

We collapsed against the wall, both of us laughing like loons. When we could breathe again, we started back to the kitchen, fingers laced together. As we walked in the door, I heard the tail end of Lila's rant—which wasn't all that ranty and warmed me on the inside. "They're ridiculously cute together."

Derrick had his back to the door and didn't see us. "I haven't seen my mom this happy in a long time."

"I *am* happy, D," Eve said, squeezing my hand. I squeezed it back.

"So am I, Mom." He turned, slung an arm over Gabriela's shoulder, and she nestled into his side with a soft smile on her face. He looked down at her, kissed her temple. "Who'd have thought I'd find the woman of my dreams at work half a world away?"

"*Someone* thinks it's not wise to fish in the company pond," Eve responded.

Lila and Rissa answered as one. "Mom."

"Though she broke *that* rule," Lila added. "With a sledgehammer."

The thought was uncomfortable, considering the meeting we were having on Monday. I shifted restlessly and slid a glance at Eve.

She leaned close, murmured in my ear. "Not today, Tal. We worry about it next week. Today, we're just like every other couple."

Not today. Good reminder. "Dinner will be ready around one, one thirty. Soup's ready now if you want to start eating." I pointed to the other things we'd put out. "We pretty much eat all day long."

"It smells so good in here, Talia," Gabriela said. "The food isn't too bad on base, but it's not home-cooked. Thank you for having us over."

Derrick agreed, helping himself to the cheese and crackers, along with smoked salmon and fresh vegetables. "Thanks for the invite. It's good to be out of BDUs for a while, not looking over my shoulder." He handed his fiancée his plate, then pulled his mother in for a hug. "I missed you, Mama."

There was a sheen of tears in Eve's eyes. "I missed you too, baby," she said, putting her hands on his cheeks, drawing him close to kiss his forehead. She sucked in a deep breath, glanced my way for the briefest of moments. "I feel better knowing you have someone there with you, looking out for you, while you're away." She turned to Gabriela, her face serious. "Thank you."

The young woman beamed. "You're welcome, Eve. Papa says the same, though he's only met Derrick on Skype."

"He's gonna kill me," Derrick muttered. "Not real happy we got engaged without him meeting me first."

"I can't imagine," Eve drawled. I pinched her side and she narrowed her eyes at me. "Mean."

I held up my hands. "Pretty sure I heard the same sentiment from you. That's all I'm saying."

Everyone laughed, even Derrick, though he winced and scrubbed the back of his neck with his hand. "We're fixing that, okay? Mom now, and Saturday we're headed to Pennsylvania for a few days to meet Gabri's family."

I glanced at Eve, who didn't seem surprised. I'd thought they were spending their whole leave here, but they'd probably discussed it last night. "That'll be nice for them too."

Gabriela nodded. "We'll be back here midweek before we ship out. A week isn't really enough leave to see everyone, but I really wanted Papa to meet Derrick. I could have more time if I wanted to since I'm a civilian, but I'd rather be where Derrick is." She tucked into his side again, and he held her close.

Lila watched them, and I could see the wheels turning in her brain. I'd talk to her when I could get her alone for a minute. Then Rissa squeezed her hand, and I changed my mind. I'd let *them* talk later, instead of me butting into my daughter's love life.

The kids—though none of them were actually kids—grabbed plates of food and went into the family room. While we were getting everything ready earlier, my girls had hauled out several board games and card games—standard Thanksgiving entertainment for our family—and I heard them discussing which one to play first. Eve and I stayed in the kitchen for a bit as I checked on the turkey.

Derrick's voice was a low, deep rumble compared to the girls' voices. We were quiet, listening to their conversations.

After a few minutes, Eve frowned. "Is Lila okay? She's not her usual bouncy self today."

I lifted a shoulder. "I think she sees Derrick and Gabri, who appear to have a nice, steady, solid relationship, and it's making her see what she didn't have—and what she wants."

"I'd like to kick his ass."

I blinked. "Derrick's? Why?"

She scowled. "No, Ryan's. He was a dick to her. And I know I'm an overprotective mama but you were right. D did good. She's a nice girl." She waved a hand. "Woman, I know. But she loves him and he loves her. That much is obvious. I was worried she was looking for someone to take care of her. Yeah, she leans on him, but not because she can't stand on her own. Because she knows he's there for her."

I put the oven mitts down and pulled Eve close, enjoying her body pressed against mine. We were silent for a bit as I kissed along her jaw and neck. I pulled back, kissed the tip of her nose. "It's good that you recognize that. That I'm right, I mean." I grinned when she snapped her teeth at me. "Mmmm. You can do that later."

"Incoming," Derrick said. "My mom's girlfriend talking about gettin' busy with my mama. I'll take *Things I don't want to hear* for $500, Alex."

Eve threw an oven mitt at him. "It's not like you weren't all over Gabri at breakfast."

He rolled his eyes. "That's different. You're my *mother*."

I laughed at the expression on his face, but I was curious. "Would it be different if I was a man?"

He snorted. "Mama's been gay my whole life, so no. Just . . . she's my mother." He put a few more appetizers on his plate, kissed us both on our cheeks, then walked out, calling down the hallway. "You're not kidding, Lila. They are all *over* each other."

This set us off again. I slung an arm around Eve's waist. "I like him, babe. He's protective of you."

"He grew up okay, didn't he? Wasn't sure either one of us would survive him being a teenager, but he's a good man. He told me last night he's up for promotion to captain. I'm so proud of him."

"You should be."

Rissa poked her head in the kitchen door. "Are you coming, or what?"

Snickers came from behind her, and my youngest daughter turned bright red. I had to stifle my laughter, as did Eve. "Be there in a minute, honey. Just grabbing food."

The minute she was out the door, Eve and I lost it again. "Good lord, Tal. They are as bad as we are." She took a bowl and ladled some soup in, then grabbed a plate and took veggies and dip and salmon.

"Where do you think they got it from?" I took some soup too, but skipped everything else. "You need to pace yourself."

She laughed, then leaned over and kissed me. "I do. I've been ordered to my brother's for dessert. You're coming with me, right? The girls are invited too."

"I think they're going to Noah's house to see their cousins, but yeah. I'll come with you."

She kissed me again. "Good."

Two hours later, when my girls finally went off to visit with their father's side of their family, Eve tossed Derrick her car keys. "Don't speed. I'll see you at Uncle Byron's house. We won't all fit in my car."

He snagged them out of the air. "Come on, baby," he said to Gabri. "Let's see how fast we can get this Matchbox car going."

Eve propped her hands on her hips. "Derrick Poe, don't you even dare. I have to work in this city."

"Bye, Mama," he called out over his shoulder, his wide grin playful and his eyes laughing.

"That boy," Eve muttered, but her face glowed with love.

"Is teasing the hell out of you because he can," I said, completely understanding her desire to smack him upside the head even though we knew he was kidding. "But yeah, doesn't matter how grown up they get, does it? They'll always be our babies."

"Amen to that." She looked around the kitchen, at the dishes in the sink and still on the table, wincing. She went to grab some plates, but I waved her off.

"I'll get them later." I stalked her, backing her up against the counter like she always did to me. "Did you notice the house is empty? No kids. Just us. And an open invitation to stop at your brother's whenever."

A smile quirked the corner of her mouth. "Do you *actually* have any energy left after all that food? Because I'm pretty much comatose."

"Mmm. I always have energy for this." I dragged her toward the bedroom, only stopping when she stood in front of the bed. "All you have to do is lie down and think of England."

She threw her head back and laughed. "Nut."

I slid her silky skirt up to her waist and pushed her onto the bed, then knelt up on the floor with my face between thighs that had spread in anticipation. I fingered the thin scrap of bronze silk that covered her mound and discovered it was a thong. "Sexy."

"Decadent. Wanted to see if you'd notice."

"Knew I couldn't keep my hands to myself, did you?"

She smiled, and it zinged me in that way her smiles always did. "Was hoping, anyway."

I stripped them off her in under a second. "A safe bet." I covered her with my mouth, plunged my tongue inside her without warning, and her head fell back as she groaned.

"God, Tal."

I tongued her for a long while, adding fingers and stroking her inside and out until she was a seething mass of need. But I didn't want her to go over this way. "Shift up on the bed," I murmured.

While she did, I stripped off my own clothes, enjoying the look of utter lust on her face when she saw my new lace underthings. I stripped them off too, then climbed on the bed and straddled one of her thighs. Holding her gaze, I unbuttoned her blouse, slowly enough that she growled at me, which made me smile. Underneath it was a thin wisp of a bra in the same gorgeous bronze that looked lovely against her skin. "Beautiful," I said, my voice thick with need I didn't bother to hide. I helped her out of it, grazing my fingers against her skin. Finally, she was naked except for her skirt, which was rucked up against her waist. I should probably have let her take it off, but I liked the rumpled look of it. Erotic. Enticing.

Mine.

I slid higher on her thigh and hooked her leg up over my shoulder, supported by my arm. As I stroked the inside of her silky thigh, I rocked against her, our mounds rubbing together. The friction was glorious, and when Eve slid a hand around my hips to grab my ass, I lost my rhythm for a moment. "Bad Eve."

"Me?" she asked, her voice husky as I slipped a hand between us, fingering her clit. "Bad Talia."

"You like me this way." She strained toward me when I lifted my fingers to my mouth and sucked on them. "I'm glad, because I've always run hot."

"Lucky me," she said on a groan as I tucked two fingers inside her, and then three. "So good."

I alternated grinding against her with fucking her until she was close, and then I moved my hand and lightly pinched her nipple, pressing so tightly against her that *her* fingers slipped inside me from behind. With my other hand, I squeezed the soft flesh of her thigh and she cried out, dragging me over the edge with her.

When we had the energy to move, we lay side by side on the bed together, chests heaving.

"Good lord." Eve bit at the side of my jaw. "One of these days you might kill me, but it'll totally be worth it."

"It's not like you don't do the same to me." I wrapped my fingers around her hip, dug them into her ass. "Your skirt is going to be a wreck."

She laughed, low and throaty. "Oh, you think so, do you? I've got your number now. I made sure to wear the one I travel with—you can wad it into a ball and it still doesn't wrinkle."

"That sounds like a dare."

She rolled off the bed and stood, shimmying it down around her hips, sans panties. "See?"

I smiled. "Sorry, babe. I think your skirt is broken."

She stared down at the definite wrinkles. "Well, hell."

"Come here." I scrambled to the side of the bed on my knees. She came close, and I tugged the skirt off, nuzzling her belly as I did it. "We'll throw it in the dryer for a few minutes."

She stepped out of it and bent over to get it. When she did, I bit her ass.

She yelped. "Warn a girl, Tal." She stood, looked at my face and laughed. "Nuh-uh. You are *not* convincing me to go for round two. No way."

I flopped onto the bed and flung my hand over my forehead dramatically. "Fine. But don't blame me if we don't get any time alone together for the next week."

After rounds two *and* round three, we didn't get to her brother's house until almost six. Derrick took one look at Eve's face and then mine, and laughed ruefully. "Two *hours?*"

I felt the blush stain my cheeks, but Eve gave him the eye. "D, I love you, but I'm pretty sure you don't want me to answer that. Not honestly, anyway."

He coughed into his hand. "True that." He nodded into the living room. "They're dying to meet Talia, and if they give you anything like the grilling Gabri and I got, you might want to turn around now."

Eve snorted. "They can try." She kissed him, then grabbed my hand and pulled me into the dining room and introduced me to everyone.

Her brother, Byron, was tall and thin and scholarly looking. Eve had told me he was a history professor at the college where we'd gone to the concert. His wife, Annette, was shorter and heavily pregnant with what Eve had said was their fourth child. Their older kids were eleven and eight and five, all boys. Eve had said this baby was a girl. Annette's family was here, her parents and siblings. Eve's sister Renee and husband were here too. The house was filled with children's happy laughter, a football game on in the other room, and the mouthwatering scent of Thanksgiving dinner.

Even though we'd eaten just a few hours ago, the smells were so divine that my stomach growled. I flushed, but Eve laughed softly, whispered in my ear. "Worked up an appetite, did you?"

"Maybe?"

In spite of Derrick's warning, the questions weren't intrusive or unwelcome. There were a few comments along the way when I turned down the ham and explained I was Jewish, but the only thing that made me truly uncomfortable was when Byron gave Eve grief about sleeping with the person who worked for her.

"Look, I know you mean well, but I can handle this," Eve said quietly to him. She reached out under the table, squeezed my hand. "*We* can handle this. And this isn't the time, okay? Not today. Please."

He agreed to let it go, but the food I'd been nibbling turned to a rock in my stomach as conversations ebbed and flowed around me. Every so often, Eve glanced over at me and I squeezed her hand, but I wasn't able to relax anymore.

I'd been trying so hard not to think about Monday, but now I couldn't think about anything else.

Chapter
THIRTEEN

Monday morning, I dressed with particular care, making sure to look professional. I hadn't seen Eve since late Thursday night, though we'd talked or texted every day. She'd spent Friday with Derrick and the weekend doing errands, and I'd spent some one-on-one time with Rissa before she headed back to college. I'd dropped her off at the train station on my way to work, and now my heart was both full and empty.

Seated at my desk, I stared at the clock. It was nearly nine, when Eve and I were supposed to meet with the chief. I'd only met him twice and, while he seemed like a nice enough guy, he also didn't seem like one to take any shit from those under his command.

My stomach knotted. Where the hell was Eve?

Another five minutes passed, and I decided I couldn't wait for her. I took the stairs instead of the elevator, needing the exercise to bleed off the adrenaline swirling in my belly. I found my way to his office.

His assistant motioned me to a chair. "He'll be with you in a moment."

As I sat, I glanced around the small office and tried not to panic. One wall held pictures of Chief Robinson at community events. Another held photos of old-time police vehicles and officers. I resisted the urge to get up and examine them and instead twisted my hands in my lap.

The assistant's computer beeped, and he looked down and then up, his face expressionless. "The chief will see you now."

"Thank you," I said to the young man, and I went in.

I stopped dead in my tracks. Eve was already there, seated in one of the chairs opposite the man's desk. Tension vibrated off her body, and she wasn't smiling. *Oy, this can't be good.*

He stood, held out a hand to me. "Talia."

I wiped my sweaty palm on my trousers and shook. "Chief Robinson."

"Lieutenant Poe is going to wait outside for a few moments while we talk alone." His voice was firm yet not hard but, at his statement, Eve stood and left the room as though she'd been shot out of a cannon.

She didn't even look at me, and I didn't know whether to laugh or cry, so I did neither and tried to control my rapidly accelerating heart rate.

When she'd closed the door behind her, he motioned to the other guest chair. I sat, my knees squeezed tight to keep them from knocking together. I expected him to sit at his desk, but instead he came around it and took the seat that Eve had vacated.

In any other circumstance, his warm gaze and steady voice would've calmed me, but this wasn't a normal meeting. "I wanted to talk with you before we all talk together. I don't like having to interfere in people's personal lives, but I will if the work of this department might be undermined. I understand you and Lieutenant Poe are in a sexual relationship?"

I swallowed and fought the urge to look away. "Yes, we are."

"And is this relationship consensual?"

I reared back as though he'd hit me. "Excuse me?"

A slight smile. "That's nearly as good as an actual answer, but I need the words. Talia, you weren't coerced into having sex with the lieutenant so you didn't lose your job, were you?"

"What? No! Not even a tiny bit," I said, aware my voice was tinged with anger I didn't try to hide. "Eve isn't that kind of person. Surely you know that."

To my surprise—considering he'd voiced the question in the first place—he nodded. "I agree with you. But I had to ask." He held up a hand when I opened my mouth to speak. "I've known Lieutenant Poe a long time, and I asked her here early so we could have a similar discussion in private. To be bluntly honest, there are some people in the ranks both higher and lower than her who take issue with a woman, a gay Black woman at that, on the job. Especially one in a command position." His face hardened. "Those people will talk. And I want to be prepared to shoot them down."

Some of my ire eased. "Neither one of us expected this."

He nodded. "That's what Eve said. She also said you're good at your job, and people who can handle the chaos of it are few and far between. She's requested a transfer to a different department to keep you there."

I blanched. "No! We talked about that. I won't let her."

He went to the door and opened it, motioning Eve back in. She stepped in and looked at me, her face pinched tightly.

I glared at her. "No. I'll quit right now. This is your *career*, damn it. I told you that. You've spent too much time building it."

"Tal . . ."

The door closed behind her and the chief spoke sharply. "Sit. Both of you."

We sat, but I glared at Eve again.

"No one is quitting." His voice drew both our gazes. "And no one needs to change jobs, as long as you two can keep it professional in the office." When Eve started to speak, he talked over her, the authority in his voice unmistakable. "Lieutenant Poe, I didn't ask your opinion."

That shut her up.

"You are not the only couple in this department. You are not the only same-sex couple in this department. But you are the only two who are in a direct command and subordinate position, and that is the issue here. You report directly to me already, Lieutenant, so that will not change. But Talia will also report directly to me now rather than to you. Talia's performance appraisals will come from me. Raises or not will come from me."

I was the one who spoke. "But, sir, you don't—"

He smiled almost gently. "I already know the kind of work you do. Eve is right. It's a job that requires a certain type of person, and we're lucky to have found you. Every cop who's dealt with you since you got here has had nothing but nice things to say." His smile to Eve was a bit sharper. "And you. If you think you're that easily replaced, that just any cop can do your job, you're out of your mind. I don't give a rat's ass that you prefer women over men in your bed.

What matters is that you care about the community we serve, and that you do your job. You do both, exceptionally well. And, maybe even more importantly, the community we all serve respects you. I've seen that over and over again. You're going nowhere, Poe."

He leaned back, pinned both of us with a hard, commanding stare for a very long, uncomfortable moment. "All of that being said, if you screw around on department time, you're *both* done. I've given this same warning to every couple in the department. Is that understood?"

Eve nodded stiffly. "Yes, sir."

It wasn't easy to get past the lump in my throat, but I did. "Yes."

"Dismissed."

We left his office in silence. So many emotions swirled through me. Relief that I wouldn't have to leave this job that I loved. Anger at Eve's high-handedness. More relief that this awkward, embarrassing *just-let-me-fall-through-the-floor* meeting was over.

We got back to our office and I grabbed my mug, heading for the break room without another word. Eve followed me, filled her own mug with hot water, then walked beside me back to the office.

I sat down, ignoring her. Hard to believe that meeting had taken less than half an hour. I felt like I'd been run through, and I was already drained.

She took a sip of her tea, watched me over the rim of her mug. "Are you going to sulk all day?"

"Yes."

She sighed. "I did what I thought was best."

That got me. "Best for who, Eve? You knew how I felt about this. I've worked here for a few months. If I needed to, I could find another job. It wouldn't be easy and money would be tight, but I'd do it. This job is your *life*. It's not what you do. It's who you are." I blew out a breath. "Not doing this. Not now. Not here, while people are watching."

She looked like she wanted to say something, but instead she honored my wish and dove into her work. I was grateful but also perversely annoyed. Which pissed me off.

We had a series of events scheduled for the school year, so I focused on the things I needed to do for the next one, which would be held in three weeks at a nearby elementary school. Or tried to, anyway—no one I needed to speak with was available. I made typos on the flier, including the department's name, for fuck's sake. Then I dropped the box of giveaways on the floor. They went rolling everywhere, even through the open door and into the hallway.

Swearing under my breath, I got on the floor and started picking them up. Tears burned my eyes, but they weren't because I was upset. I was *angry*. At myself, at Eve, and the whole damn situation.

I was nearly in the hall when someone held out one of the stress balls to me. I looked up to find Delia there, a grin on her face. It faded when she saw my eyes. "You okay?"

I blinked away the tears and gritted my teeth. "Yeah, just clumsy." I stood, took the ball, and turned to go back inside when I felt her hand on my elbow.

"Take a walk with me?" Delia asked.

I glanced back over my shoulder. Eve's face held that pinched look again, but God help me, I needed to be away from her before I said something I'd regret. "Sure."

"I'll have your assistant back in ten," she told Eve, and then she led me to a part of the building I'd never seen before. She grinned faintly at my confusion. "I grew up haunting the hallways here—my dad was a cop too. I know where all the good hiding places are."

We went into a small room. It was jam-packed with dusty filing cabinets, a microfilm reader, and a few other things straight out of the last century. I sneezed, and my already-watery eyes overflowed. "Where are we?"

"Records room for cases prior to 1970." There were two metal chairs and an industrial table in the center of the room. She pulled out a chair and sat, gesturing to the other. "Looked like you needed an escape route before you blew up or melted down."

I gave a somewhat choked laugh. "That obvious?"

She smiled wryly. "To someone who has a similar temperament? Yeah. You need to chill before you speak?"

"*Ding ding ding.*"

"I figured. It's the thing about me that makes Colin the craziest, but at least he gets it now." She rubbed her burgeoning belly. "Need an impartial ear to talk about whatever's bothering you?"

I considered her offer, and dismissed it. "As tempting as that is, it's probably better I don't."

"Fair enough," she said, and the look on her face should've warned me what was coming next. "Rumor has it you and Eve were in the chief's office this morning, and that you two are a couple."

"Oh, hell. Everyone knows?"

"Yup. This place is lousy for gossip. Can I give you a piece of free advice?"

Like I could stop her? I lifted a shoulder. "Go for it."

"Don't let them get to you. I dealt with a lot of bullshit at the beginning of my career because I'm the chief's niece. Ignore them, and they'll go away."

I blinked. "He's your uncle?"

"He is. My point is, do your job and people will forget about the rest." She rubbed her belly again, then checked her watch. "We have four more minutes before Eve comes after us."

"I need to head back, anyway." I wiped under my eyes. "And for the record, I wasn't upset. I was mad."

She grinned and patted her red hair. "Don't I know how that goes. Doesn't seem fair, does it? Colin just yells. I implode, and it's never pretty."

That made me laugh. "I can relate. Does anyone ever come in here anymore?"

"Believe it or not, yes. Every once in a while, a new detective is assigned cold cases to work on. Or a name comes up that some old-timer remembers from way back when and they need a case file." She looked around. "It'd be great to get it computerized for ease of searches, but there's something to be said for searching in old, dusty files. I like it as it is." She checked her watch again. "Time's up."

On our way back, I took some deep breaths and tried to put myself into a better frame of mind for work. What I'd told Eve wasn't wrong. Our personal shit had to wait.

We reached the end of the hallway and Delia turned left while I turned right, but not before she gave me a conspiratorial nudge. "You've got this."

"Thanks." I smiled weakly, then walked the short distance to mine and Eve's office.

I half expected her to be pacing the room, but instead she was at her desk, the phone to her ear. Her replies were short . . . *yes, uh-huh, sure.* I sat down and watched her work, this woman I was pretty sure I was falling in love with, even though I wanted to strangle her.

She finished her call and looked at me, her expression that carefully blank cop face. "Better?"

My heart twisted at the distance in her eyes. "Some. But we need to talk when we get home."

"It's Monday. You have your class tonight," she reminded me.

Shit, I'd forgotten all about it in the stress of this morning's meeting. "I'll cancel."

Eve shook her head. "No. It's important to you."

Frustration ate at me. "*You're* important to me, and we need to talk. I'll cancel."

"Funny how that works," Eve muttered. "When I did what I thought was best, you didn't like it."

I opened my mouth to retort, then snapped it shut because she might be right but, damn it, she was still wrong in trying to make huge unilateral decisions that affected both of us. I leaned back in my chair, crossed my arms over my chest. "Are we having our first fight?"

She leaned back in her own chair. "Seems like it."

"Fine."

"Fine."

The rest of the morning dragged, and I was grateful when Eve got called away to a meeting. I felt miserable, but at least this silence wasn't deafening. By the time I left for the day, she still wasn't back.

I was torn between leaving her a note or not, but decided I didn't want to, not in the office where anyone could see it, especially after today. And really, I didn't know what to say. I was upset that she'd requested to change jobs after I'd specifically told her I hated that idea, and yeah, I was mad. I hadn't felt this way in a long time. Being at odds with my lover was every bit as awful as I'd remembered.

I headed home and canceled my class because my heart wasn't in it after the day I'd had. I checked my phone every few minutes to see if I had any texts from Eve, but there was nothing.

I made myself eat something and then, before I could change my mind, drove over to Eve's duplex. The lights were off, and the driveway was empty. She'd loaned Derrick and Gabriela her car for their trip to Pennsylvania, and the cruiser she was using while they were gone wasn't there.

Damn it.

I called her. It rang several times, and I was sure she would let it go to voicemail but then she picked up.

"Eve? Where are you? I'm at your house. I wanted to talk about today."

"Hey," she said, sounding tired and distant and not her usual self. "I'm not there. One of the guys who does PAL stuff had a conflict and asked me to cover for him. I'm at the community center for another few hours."

That explained all the noise in the background.

There was a loud crash and then a shriek, and Eve swore under her breath. "I've gotta go break up a fight. I'll see you tomorrow, okay?"

My stomach rolled over. "Babe, we need to talk about this."

She blew out a tight gust of air. "I . . . Not tonight, Talia."

And then she was gone. I took a few breaths, tried to think. I could push the issue, stay here and wait for her to get home, or I could give her the space she wanted. I knew the right thing to do—give her room—but anxiety roiled in my gut. I sat there for a good fifteen minutes arguing with myself before exhaustion rolled over me, and my decision was made. Though my heart was heavy, I started my car, then drove home.

I slept badly. I missed Eve in my bed, and hated that we were at odds, especially over something so stupid. It had taken several hours of insomnia for my anger to bleed off, to realize that, once again, I was mad at her for a dumb reason. She cared enough about me to step away from a job she loved, and I'd done nothing but give her grief. She shouldn't have made that sacrifice, and definitely not without telling me what she'd planned first, but I sure as hell shouldn't have been fighting with her because she'd offered to. Especially after the chief had turned her down flat.

Bleary-eyed though I was, I rolled out of bed when the alarm went off, showered, and got dressed for work. I wanted to see Eve, to apologize for the way I'd handled things, but I had a stop I needed to make first.

I'd found Lila's inhaler in Rissa's room last night as I'd wandered the house like a zombie. She had another but liked to have two, in case one didn't work. As her mom and someone who'd sat through far too many ER visits, shaking with fear for my baby, I liked her to have two also. I went to her apartment to drop it off, but she wasn't home, so I went to Noah's office and he sent me to her job site. Once there, I handed it over and, to her utter dismay, gave her a kiss on the forehead in front of her coworker—who happened to be her cousin. She cocked her head at me, frowned.

"You okay, Mom? You seem worried."

"I'm fine, sweetie. Better now that I know you have this."

She looked skeptical, my sensitive child, but nodded and tucked the inhaler in her back pocket. "I'll call you tonight?"

"Sounds good, honey."

Back at work, I pulled into the parking lot and my cell phone went off. I recognized it as the police station's main number, and I frowned. Had Eve forgotten her phone?

I answered as I got out of the car. "I know I'm late, sorry. I'm just on my way in the door."

"Talia, it's Chief Robinson. I need to have a word with you."

My heart flipped over. Had someone heard our argument yesterday and ratted on us? Already? "Sir, I promise you, we haven't—"

"Not about that. I need you to come directly to your office, please."

Something in his tone was off, and even as I wondered about his odd request, the employee door opened and Delia strode out, her face tight as she walked toward me. I recognized that serious, solemn look, had seen it only once before in my life on the day police officers had informed me my husband was dead.

"Eve," I breathed, and a buzzing noise started in my head as my heart revved into overdrive. "No. *No.*"

Chapter
FOURTEEN

"**S**he's alive," Delia said immediately, taking me by the arm and quickly ushering me inside, around a handful of people standing near our office door, talking in hushed tones. They went silent as I passed by.

Chief Robinson was on the phone, leaning against Eve's desk, his pose rigid rather than relaxed. "Whoever you need. Just find the son of a bitch," he barked, and shoved the phone in his pocket. He looked at me and swore under his breath. "Sit down before you fall down."

"No. Tell me," I demanded, trying to breathe, trying to hold on to the fact that she was alive. Not dead, like Seth. *Alive.* I was shaking, and sitting was probably a good idea, but if Eve was alive, I needed to see her and I needed to see her *now*. "What happened?"

He exhaled sharply. "As far as we can tell, she was shot three times. Once in her arm, twice in her chest, all at close range. She's been flown to Shock Trauma for surgery."

My head spun and then next thing I knew I was in a chair. My mind filled with images of caskets and funerals, a mixture of Seth and Eve, and then I couldn't breathe at all. *I can't do this again. I can't. Please, God, don't take her away from me.* A hand pushed at my back until I was folded in half with my head hanging between my knees.

"Breathe, Talia. Slow, deep breaths."

Delia kept talking to me and rubbing my back. I didn't know for how long, but finally my lungs eased open and though I wanted to be sick, I fought it back. "Derrick. I need to tell Eve's son."

Chief Robinson nodded. "We're covering that, but if I recall, he's serving overseas so it may take a while."

I shook my head. "He's here on leave for Thanksgiving. In Pennsylvania until tomorrow, meeting his future in-laws. And Eve's parents and sisters and brother need to know before they find out from someone else." My hands shook as I tried to use my phone. "I have to call Derrick." He'd given me his number on Thanksgiving, since *you're a big part of Mama's life.* "I need to—"

Delia gently took the phone from me and dialed, then handed it back.

Derrick answered immediately. "Yo, Talia. I'm glad you called. I tried to get Mama but she's not answering so I guess she's busy. We're going to stay here another day."

My throat choked with tears. "You need to come home right now. She's in surgery. She . . . she was shot this morning."

Shocked silence, then an expletive. "Details," he demanded, his voice sharpening to that of a trained Marine.

I tried getting them out, but didn't do such a great job of it. Someone took my phone again, and I heard Chief Robinson explaining the situation to Derrick. I sat there, my mind whirling with awful, horrible possibilities, and then he handed the phone back to me. As he did, I heard Derrick yelling for Gabriela. "We'll drive straight through to Baltimore and meet you at the hospital," he told me. "We should be there in about two and a half hours. Gabriela's going to drive while I call my grandparents and my aunts and uncles and fill them in."

Two and a half hours seemed awfully fast. "Be careful, honey."

He agreed, then disconnected. Dear God, I needed to call my own girls so they knew before it hit the news. I needed to get to the hospital too, and how was I going to—

"You'll ride with me," Chief Robinson said, as though he'd read my mind. Or maybe I'd said it out loud, I didn't know. "I'm headed there now. You can call your daughters while we're on the way." He put a hand on my shoulder, handed me some tissues. "Let's go."

Once we were on the road, I called Lila and explained the situation to her. I was crying and she was crying and I told her to tell Noah she needed to be taken off jobs today. Working with electricity required concentration, and I didn't need to worry about her too. Then I called Rissa, who said she'd be okay and did I want her to come home. Her voice was small and worried and I wished I could hug her, hug both my girls, but I said no and told her to be with her friends today, to call me if she needed me.

Chief Robinson stayed quiet as I finished up my calls, but I could see his cold fury in the stony set of his jaw. A muscle pulsed in his cheek as he got continuous updates on the police radio in the car and translated them into plain English for me. I learned the whole sequence of the morning's horrible events as we drove the almost-hour to Baltimore, and they made me want to vomit.

Early in the morning, a man had walked up to a female sheriff's deputy who'd been sitting in her cruiser outside a convenience store in the neighboring county, and shot her in the head. He'd fled, and a BOLO had been put out for him, along with a description of his car.

Dispatch stated that Eve had spotted the car crossing the intersection where she'd been stopped for a red light and called it in, requesting backup but stating that she was following.

A few minutes after that, someone had called 911 after seeing a car fleeing the scene and an officer lying in the street, bleeding. The witness had been able to provide more information about the car and the direction it was traveling, and a roadblock had been set up.

The suspect had driven directly into one of two Maryland State Police cruisers that were blocking the road. He'd passed the car with the male driver and rammed into the one with the female Trooper so hard he'd pushed it into a tree. She'd been pinned in her cruiser and was also in surgery at the same hospital as Eve.

He'd kept driving, and there was a manhunt underway for him now.

About forty-five minutes later, we pulled into a small parking lot near the back of the hospital, alongside quite a few different law enforcement cars. The sun was bright and it was a clear, beautiful day . . . much like the day I'd lost Seth.

Tears threatened again but I forced them back. There was no time for me to fall apart, not when Eve needed me.

We were met at the door and ushered through to a small surgical waiting area that was empty but for two cops with grim faces. Chief Robinson gave them a curt nod but didn't say anything else as he nudged me none-too-gently into a chair.

"Stay here while I get an update."

I waited, my arms curled around my waist as he went back out into the hall, and prayed like I'd never prayed before.

I got a few curious looks from the cops, but their attention was diverted when a distraught young man carrying a little boy raced into the room, followed by a dark-haired man in a Maryland State Trooper's uniform with his hat tucked under his arm. The boy's brown eyes were wide as saucers, and he clung to his father like a burr. It only took a few minutes for me to realize this man must be related to the Trooper who'd been pinned in her car by the same man who'd shot Eve. I sent up another prayer for the young woman also in surgery.

Chief Robinson came back in the room, his face granite, and my stomach turned over. "Tell me," I demanded.

"The bullet in her arm nicked an artery and she lost a lot of blood. They were able to staunch it and gave her a transfusion on the flight, but she coded once on the way here. One of the bullets to her chest did a lot of internal damage, and they are doing what they can. She likely also has a concussion, since she hit her head as she fell. That's all they could tell me."

I started trembling and could not stop. Someone sat beside me and placed a warm blanket around my shoulders. I blinked, looked over at him. He seemed familiar, but I couldn't place him. "T-thank you."

When Delia came in carrying a vending cup, it clicked. This was her husband. She took the seat on the other side of me and held out the cup. "Coffee, if you'd like." I shook my head no and she set it down, then took my hand and squeezed. "Since I'm still on limited duty, I volunteered to sit with you while you wait, and Colin is off duty today."

I squeezed her hand back, cleared my throat "Thanks."

Colin stood and went over to Chief Robinson, who stood with the Troopers. He shook hands with the dark-haired man who looked as furious as the chief had earlier.

"That's Lieutenant Alex Meyers. He's the Maryland State Police barracks commander for our area, and the Trooper who was injured is under his command," Delia said. "Nice guy, great cop. He and his wife, Jess, are friends of ours."

I knew she was trying to keep me occupied with random conversation, but my mind would not stop spinning. "I . . . I can't stop thinking the worst."

Her smile was gentle as she squeezed my hand again. "Understandable, but Eve's in good hands, and she's exactly where she needs to be."

I knew that, and I was trying to think positively, but I also knew about regrets. After my last fight with Seth, I'd slept with my back to him all night. I'd still been in a funk the next morning and had pulled out of his arms, because why not? We'd fought before, and we'd worked it out each time. But then he was gone, forever gone, and I couldn't ever fix it. It was one of my deepest regrets.

Here I was again, and history was repeating itself. My eyes burned. If Eve died—

A surgeon came out of the double doors, and everyone turned. "Trooper Ruiz's family?"

I sagged as the young man came forward, wearing the same fear on his face that had to be on mine. "I—I'm Isabella's husband, Antonio." The surgeon tried to lead him to a private room, but he squared his shoulders and shook his head, gesturing to the cops, one of whom was holding the little boy. "No. Tell me here. They're her family too."

"The crash broke both her legs and she suffered several broken ribs. One of them ruptured her spleen, which I removed. The orthopedic surgeon is still setting her fractures. That will take a while, but she's stable. She's a very lucky young woman, considering what happened. She's going to have a long recovery ahead of her, but she's strong."

The relief on her husband's face was profound. "Thank you. Thank you."

Not long after that, Trooper Ruiz's family went up to ICU, leaving us the only ones in the waiting room.

A cell phone buzzed. Lieutenant Meyers, who was still standing with Chief Robinson, answered it. After the conversation, his face was grimly satisfied. "Got him. He ditched the car and fled on foot, so we sent up the helo to search. They cornered him in a strip mall. He's in custody now. I'm going upstairs to give Ruiz the news."

He and the chief stepped into the hall, but even though his voice was low, I heard the rest. "He hasn't stopped bragging about how he taught those *bitch cops* a lesson just like he'd said he was going to."

I flinched at the vicious words, but my heart jolted and I caught Delia's eyes as they went wide.

She swore out loud. "Christ. The guy the emails warned us about, the one who tagged those cruisers? I need to get our case notes to the MSP, and I want to be in on that interview." She followed after them even as she was dialing her phone.

Conversation ebbed and flowed around me, and I lost track of time, staring at those double doors. I wasn't sure how long I sat there, waiting, but it had to have been quite a while because suddenly Derrick was in front of me, pulling me to my feet and squeezing me in a giant bear hug.

He looked haggard. "Any word on my mother?"

Chief Robinson came over, shook Derrick's hand. "No, but I'd think soon. And so you know, the bastard who did this to her is in custody."

"Good. But why wasn't she in a vest?" Derrick asked. "She always wears her body armor when she's working."

I hadn't thought about that, and he was right, but I knew her daily routine. "She comes to work, then runs, showers, and dresses for the day. She was on her way in when it happened."

Since I was up, I started pacing. Delia was back in the room and leaning against Colin, who had his hand cupped over her slightly rounded stomach. The chief was talking to them. Derrick was pacing too, like a caged panther. Gabriela watched him with worried eyes that were red from crying. Every time I passed Derrick on my lap around the room, I rubbed my hand against his back.

The double doors pushed open and a surgeon came out, rolling his shoulders and neck as if to work out the kinks in them. We all froze where we were. "Lieutenant Poe's family?"

Derrick grabbed my hand and pulled me forward. "How's my mother?"

"In critical condition." He scrubbed a hand over the back of his neck. "She was lucky the medevac carries blood products. Without that on-board transfusion, she might not have made it. She coded once on the flight but they were able to get her heart going again. We repaired the damage to her artery, and it should be fine. One of the bullets to her chest broke a rib, which punctured her lung and lodged in the chest cavity. The other one ricocheted off another rib and traveled through her stomach and large intestine. We've repaired everything we could see, but there could be more that we missed. She's being moved to ICU now." The phone clipped to his scrubs buzzed, and he nodded sharply, then headed back through the double doors.

I felt faint. How could one person survive that much damage? Derrick put his arm around me, and I sagged against him, holding him tightly. "I'm sorry," I whispered. "I'm so sorry. We had a fight after our meeting with the chief yesterday, and she went home. If she'd been at my house, maybe . . ."

He hugged me closer. "Don't do this to yourself. If I've learned anything in the Marines, what-ifs after the fact will make you crazy. Mama would tell you that herself." He frowned down at me, then looked over at the chief. "What meeting?"

"About our relationship, and the fact that Eve's my boss."

"*Was* your boss," Chief Robinson said. "You report to me now, remember?"

I nodded, and he went back over to sit with Delia and Colin again.

Derrick squeezed me. "What happened?"

"Someone found out we were seeing each other and tried to make trouble for us. So she tried to protect me by putting in a transfer request after we'd talked about it and I'd told her that I hated the idea."

He sighed. "That's my mama, stubborn to the bone."

Gabriela had been standing there silently, but now she spoke, leaning into Derrick's side. "That's what's going to get her through this, you know."

From your mouth to God's ear.

The nurse, a young blonde woman wearing a thick cross on a chain around her neck, wouldn't let me into the ICU. She blocked the door, arms crossed, and glared down her nose at me. "Husband or children only."

I reared back, stunned, never imagining this scenario. I didn't know what to say, was struck speechless, but it turned out I didn't have to say anything.

Derrick grabbed my hand and pulled me forward with him. "I'm her son, but I have two mothers. My mom needs to see my mama, and you are going to move your homophobic ass out of the way so that can happen." At six feet tall, with his Marine bearing, he was an imposing presence. "I don't care what your personal beliefs are, but we are family. *Move*."

Another nurse came over to see what the issue was. Chief Robinson took her aside, and within two minutes, I was standing next to the bed where Eve lay, still except for the rise and fall of her chest at every pump of the ventilator. Her skin had a grayish cast, and the white bandages on her arm and her chest made her look incredibly frail. Derrick made a choked noise and I squeezed him hard. Tears shimmered in his beautiful brown eyes that were so much like Eve's.

"She'll make it, honey," I said, fighting my own tears. I had to believe it, and I had to be strong. For him, for Eve, for myself. In her, I'd found a happiness and a partnership I'd never expected to find again, and I couldn't lose her. I didn't know if I could survive such a significant loss twice.

"She seems so small," he said, his voice thick. "And so still. Mama is never this still, y'know? She's always moving, doing something."

"Yeah." I leaned forward, careful of all the tubes and wires and bandages, and kissed her softly on her forehead. "Fight, babe. You have to fight. Derrick needs you. I need you. Fight, damn it."

I moved out of the way, and Derrick leaned in close as I'd had. "Don't leave me, Mama."

My heart twisted painfully.

He stood, and we held each other as the ventilator breathed for Eve, one even pump at a time.

I hadn't left the hospital in the thirty-six hours since I'd gotten here, though Chief Robinson and the Butlers had gone. Someone from the department was here all the time, keeping vigil, a fact I greatly appreciated. Eve's family was here too—her brother and her sister. Her other sister was driving their parents up from South Carolina tomorrow. They'd asked extended family to wait until she was out of ICU.

I sat in the chair next to Eve's bed in the ICU, touching her foot, one of the only parts of her not hooked up to a machine. "I made Derrick go get some dinner with Gabri. He looked like he was about to fall over." I talked to her almost constantly. I had no idea if she heard me or not, but I needed to fill up the silence so I didn't focus on the damn *beep, beep, beep* of the machines. "He didn't want to leave. He's as stubborn as you are, though I guess you already know that."

My eyes scanned her for the thousandth time, looking for any sign she was waking, but nothing.

There was the scuff of a shoe at the door, and then a muffled sob. I turned to see Lila, her eyes round and a hand covering her mouth.

"Oh, baby. Let it out." I stood and pulled my daughter into my arms, holding her until her sobs eased off and her body stopped shaking.

She took a shuddering deep breath and wiped her eyes. "Is she going to be okay?"

My stomach clenched. "They don't know yet, honey. I have to believe she will be. I have to." I squeezed Lila tightly, then sat, touching Eve's foot again. I needed that contact, to feel the warmth of her skin. I hoped she could feel it, that she knew I was there.

Lila stood beside me until a nurse came in, frowning. "There's only supposed to be one person in here at a time."

"I'll go," Lila said, her voice still unsteady. "I just needed to see my stepmom for myself. And I needed to make sure my mom was taking care of herself too."

The nurse's frown softened. "Five more minutes, okay?"

"Thanks." When the nurse left the room, Lila squeezed my shoulder, then stepped around me to the head of the bed. She laid a trembling hand lightly on the blanket covering Eve's shoulder. "You have to get better, Eve. You can do this. Mom needs you.

Derrick needs you. Rissa and I need you too." She sniffed, a half sob. "You make Mom so happy. You have to get better. You have to."

My beautiful girl with her loving heart.

Lila stood there a few more minutes, closing her eyes and bowing her head, and when she was done, she came back into my arms for a long hug. "She'll be okay, Mom. I know it."

I held her tightly and kissed the top of her head. "I hope so, honey."

It was nearly eleven, and everyone but Derrick and I had gone home to get some sleep. He was in with Eve, and I was outside talking to one of the nurses when all kinds of alarms started going off in her room. Panic clawed at me as the ICU staff raced to Eve's side, checking her vitals as well as the machines and their connections. When they called for a doctor, *stat*, I knew it had to be bad.

They'd shoved Derrick out of the small space. He stood by my side, gripping my hand as we waited. When the nurses started hooking her up to portable monitors, my chest grew tight.

The ICU doctor came over, his face grim. "Her vitals dropped below the threshold we like to see and they're still dropping, which means she's probably bleeding internally. We're taking her back down to the OR."

Derrick made a pained noise and I squeezed his hand.

We ran with the team who were hurriedly pushing Eve's bed toward the bank of elevators. Derrick let go of my hand and leaned forward to kiss his mother just as the doors whooshed open. "I love you, Mama," he said, his voice choked.

They had her inside with the doors closing before I could do the same. I blinked back the tears. I could *not* fall apart now. Could not. "Where do we wait?" I asked, though it was hard to speak.

One of the nurses who'd stayed in the ICU squeezed my arm. "Come with me. I'll get you settled."

The entire surgical waiting area was empty except for Derrick and me and a young woman pacing the hallway just outside the room.

We waited, and we waited, and we waited. Derrick called his aunts and uncle and then Gabriela, and I spoke with my girls. As we continued to wait, the young woman in the hallway went home. We made small talk and drank far too much coffee. Finally, after about four hours, a surgeon came out to talk with us.

"We found a nick in a vein that had been hidden by other damage. It's been repaired, but she needed more blood. We're keeping her here in surgical recovery for the rest of the night, in case there's anything else going on and we need to get her into the OR again. If her vitals stay stable by midmorning, we'll move her back up to ICU." The woman hesitated, then continued. "She's undergone a lot of trauma in the last day and a half. The next few hours will be critical."

She didn't have to explain what she meant, and it was obvious from the guarded expression on Derrick's face he understood.

I was exhausted, but I couldn't sleep, and I wouldn't leave. I sat sideways on one of the sofas, leaning my head against a blanket one of the nurses had given me. Derrick paced for a bit, then sat with his arms on his knees, his head in his hand. I didn't know if he was praying, so I didn't bother him until he looked up again.

His eyes were bleak. "It's bad, isn't it?"

I scooted over to him, took his big hands in mine, and squeezed. "It *is* bad, but your mother isn't giving up without a fight. She's in phenomenal shape for a woman twenty years younger than her. Plus, she's stubborn as a mule. She's not ready to go yet. She's not."

His jaw worked, and he buried his head in his hands again.

I wished I knew better how to comfort him, but I didn't, so I just rubbed his back and kept him company as we waited.

And waited.

And waited.

Chapter
FIFTEEN

I t'd been four days since Eve had been shot, four days she'd been unconscious, two days since her second surgery. Derrick was still on leave, and we'd booked a hotel room in Baltimore so we didn't have to drive back and forth every day. We took turns sitting with Eve, and he had just gone back to the hotel to grab a few hours of sleep. It was around midnight, but we refused to leave her alone, and the nursing staff knew to let me in. Derrick and Chief Robinson had made sure of that.

I talked to her constantly, both to keep myself awake and to hopefully get through to her. "You know the other cop, the Trooper whose car was rammed into a tree by the same guy who shot you? They sat her up today for the first time. She's got two broken legs and she had to have been in a lot of pain, but you should've seen her face when she got to hold her little boy. Sheer joy. You'd like her, Eve. She's stubborn, like you. You need to wake up so you can meet her."

Nothing.

My throat grew tight. Every day—hell, every hour, every minute—that went by where she remained unconscious was bad. "I've had a lot of time to think, and I know I shouldn't spring this on you while you're unconscious, but . . . I love you. I'm not sure when it happened, exactly, but there it is. I love you. You have to wake up so I can tell you when you'll remember."

Not the tiniest twitch, not a single indication that she'd heard me bare my heart.

I fought back a sob, taking several deep, shuddering breaths. She needed me to stay cool and calm and collected. "I know I told you this before, but they got the guy who did this to you. Remember the day we went to lunch at the amphitheater, and you took down the idiot who grabbed the homeless man's hat? It was him. Delia got to sit in on his interrogation yesterday, and she said he kept saying you got what you had coming to you. She and Officer Anderson were here last night, and I heard them talking about it." I rubbed the heel of my hand against my heart and kept on talking. "Turns out his ex-girlfriend is a sheriff's deputy who dumped him in public one night. He called her a *bitch cop*, and threats were tossed around. It was overheard by several homeless people who sleep under the bridges along the creek, including the person Isaiah knew. They didn't want any trouble, but they didn't want to just let it go, hence the emails. Anyway, apparently the guy tried to get back together with her, and she told him no and that if he didn't leave her alone, she'd file a restraining order. She's the officer he killed at the convenience store."

I stroked her leg, studied her face. Still nothing.

"Why didn't you wait for backup, Eve?" My throat grew tight. "You didn't have on your vest. We all know you wouldn't be careless without a good reason, and we need you to tell us why. Why did you get out of your car, knowing he'd already killed someone, knowing you weren't wearing your vest? I need you to tell me why, damn it. Why would you do something so stupid?" I started shaking and couldn't stop. "Please wake up, babe. I need you. I love you so much."

I dropped my head to the bed, my hand on her leg, struggling not to give in to the tears. I was exhausted, mentally and physically, and I wasn't sure how much more I could take before I broke into a million tiny pieces.

Several of the alarms went off, beeping and blinking. I shoved to my feet, fear clawing at me. "No," I breathed. "No, not again."

A team of nurses rushed in and pushed me out of the way until I stood just outside the cubicle. When one of them moved, I could see that Eve's eyes were open but unseeing, her face contorted and her body rigid. I sent up a fervent prayer and wrapped my arms around my waist. *Please let her be waking up. Please, God. Don't take her from me.*

"Lieutenant Poe, you need to stay still," the head nurse said, the deep baritone of his voice calm. "The ventilator is breathing for you and you need to let it. Fighting it only makes it worse. We're getting the doctor now, and as soon as she examines you and says it's okay, we'll remove the tube."

I couldn't see her face anymore, but her legs moved under the blanket.

The ICU doctor stepped into the cube and drew the curtain shut. With fear clogging my veins, I pulled out my cell and called Derrick, both my hands and my voice trembling. "She's awake."

One of the nurses who'd been so kind to me came out from behind the curtain and offered me a smile. Her father was a cop, she'd told me days ago. Retired, but she knew how hard all of this was. "It's a good sign," she said, heading back to the monitoring station. "A really good sign. Give them a few minutes."

What else could I do? Derrick arrived a few minutes later and joined me as I paced back and forth, worry and impatience warring on his handsome face. It took longer than a few minutes, more like half an hour, and by that time, we'd nearly worn a hole in the floor.

Finally, the curtain opened. Eve's ventilator had been replaced by an oxygen tube. Her eyes were closed again, but her chest rose and fell in a much more natural rhythm. As much as I wanted to see Eve, tell I loved her and I was so sorry we'd argued, as soon as the nurse signaled it was okay for one of us to go in, I pushed Derrick forward. "Go see your mother."

When he came out, he was fighting tears. I led him to a quiet alcove steps away from Eve's bed, opened my arms, and held him close, my lover's child. He shook for a moment as he got himself back under control.

"Sorry," he said, pulling back and dashing a hand under his eyes. "It's relief. I was so worried I would lose her. I know she's not out of the woods yet, but this . . . I needed this. I have my aunts and uncles and grandparents and now Gabriela, but Mama is always, *always* there for me. I don't know what I'd do without her."

I put my hand on his arm. "She loves you more than anyone in the world."

"I know," he said, unable to stop a shudder as he wiped his eyes again. "She couldn't talk, but she mouthed *I love you*. I told her I loved her too." He straightened up and slipped his arm over my shoulder, kissing my cheek. "She'll want to see you."

But when I went back, she was sleeping. I was worried at first, but she drifted in and out of incredibly short seconds of wakefulness for the next several hours, which the nurse said was fairly normal given her condition and her injuries. Derrick was still there, sleeping on the sofa in the waiting room, in case anything changed. I stayed in the room with her, lightly napping in the chair next to her bed. Around four in the morning, I jolted awake to a sound that was different than all the machine noises.

"Ta . . . l."

Eve's voice was a mere whisper but it brought me to my feet. I came close, carefully took her hand. "Babe."

"D."

Derrick. "He's here. You want me to get him?"

It was a struggle for her to speak. "Lo . . . ve."

My throat tightened at the worry in her eyes. "He knows you love him, babe. He knows. He said you told him when you woke up." A tear leaked from the corner of her eye, and I gently squeezed her fingers. "Shh. Rest, Eve. We'll be here."

Her eyes fluttered closed, and once again she succumbed to sleep.

I stepped out for a minute, stopped in the waiting room to find Derrick awake and texting. "You okay, honey?"

He stretched. "Yeah. I'm used to combat naps so those few hours were all I needed."

I came and sat beside him. He leaned back against the sofa and drew me with him, his arm over my shoulder. We both put our feet up on the coffee table. "How're you holding up, Tal?"

His use of my shortened name, the one Eve always used, warmed me. I'd only known him for a short while, but he had already claimed a piece of my heart. "Better. She woke again. Wanted me to make sure you knew she loves you." I looked up at him, once again struck by how much he resembled Eve. Masculine to her feminine, but the family resemblance couldn't be denied.

His phone dinged and he thumbed over the message, making one of those male grunts that could mean anything from *oh, shit*, to *it's about time*. "My CO approved my extended emergency leave. I have to update him daily, but right now I'm good to stay. Thank God."

I knew he'd been worried about that, and I was relieved for him. "What about Gabriela?"

"She's taking some vacation time and she'll stay here with me. She had a lot saved up." He squeezed my shoulder with his hand. "You should go back to the hotel and get some sleep. You're exhausted, and you won't do anyone any good if you get sick."

I couldn't hide my yawn. "You'll go sit with her? I don't want her alone if she wakes up again." I eyed the sofa. "I'll just rest here."

He snorted. "Does Mama know how stubborn you are?"

I smiled the first real smile I'd had in days, though it was shaky. "She does."

He snorted again and got up, handing me the pillow and blanket he'd used. "Glad to hear it. Someone needs to give her grief when I'm away."

He kissed my temple and left the room, and I drifted off to sleep.

He woke me a few hours later. "She's asking for you, Tal."

I bolted upright and stood, but I got up too fast and my head spun. "Whoa."

"Easy there," he said, steadying me. "When was the last time you ate anything?"

I thought about it. "Breakfast? Maybe? What day is it?"

He sighed. "Go see Mama, and I'll get you some food."

I went, but told him not to bother with food because I knew I wouldn't be able to eat a single bite. Eve's eyes were closed and I was afraid she'd fallen back asleep, but when I took her hand, they fluttered open. "Ta . . . l."

"I'm here, babe."

"Love . . . you."

That did it. The tears I'd managed to hold back for days spilled over. "Damn it, you beat me to it. I love you too."

"Know . . . heard." Her eyes drifted shut and her breathing evened out.

Oh, my heart. I dropped into the chair I'd spent so many hours in, not releasing her hand, my damp eyes on her face as I waited for her to wake up again. I *loved* this woman who made me feel so much more than I'd felt in years, and she loved me.

I prayed we'd get the chance to grow old together.

Over the next two days, Eve grew stronger, staying awake longer between bouts of sleep. Once again, we took turns in the ICU with her, neither of us wanting to leave her alone. While Derrick sat with her, I went back to the hotel and slept for a few hours, then showered and called my girls. I'd been keeping them as updated as best I could. We swapped on and off, but these last few days had been exhausting.

After waking up from a short nap, I went back to the hospital, meeting up with Derrick in the waiting room. "How's she doing? And why are you out here?"

He smiled tiredly. "She's cranky. They said that's good. They wanted some space to run a few tests."

"You need some sleep," I said, noting the circles under his eyes. He'd been doing double duty, sitting with his mother and ferrying his grandparents back and forth to the hospital to see Eve. "Why don't you head back to the hotel and lay down?"

"Actually, I need some exercise. I'm not used to sitting around like this. I'm going to go for a run around the harbor. Can I get you anything while I'm out?"

I shook my head. "I'm good. Be careful out there, honey."

He headed for the door, and when he reached it, he turned. The corner of his mouth quirked up in a smile so much like Eve's it made my heart ache. "Yes, Mom."

I laughed, though it sounded rusty. After a quick stop at the nurse's station, I went into Eve's room and was surprised to find her awake. "Hey there, sexy."

She tried to lick her lips. "Thir . . . sty."

The nurse who was taking her vitals shook her head. "Sorry, Lieutenant. Nothing to eat or drink yet." She took a cup and filled it with the tiniest bit of water and a sponge on a stick. She dabbed it on Eve's mouth, then handed it to me. "You can use this to wet her lips and her tongue. That should help. Not too much, though."

The nurse left the room. "More," Eve said.

"A tiny bit." I dabbed like the nurse had and put the sponge back in the cup.

Eve licked her lips. "More."

"Nope. Just a little. You heard her."

"Mean."

I laughed, relieved to be on the receiving end of her teasing, and dabbed a tiny bit more water. "Bossy."

She licked the water off her lips again. "Don't . . . forget . . . it."

"Like you'd ever let me." I slid my hand under hers on the bed, and this time, she actually gripped it. Not tightly, but it was a good sign. "I'm so sorry, Eve."

A tiny wrinkle in her brow. "Why."

"Because we fought, and over something stupid. You shouldn't have told Chief Robinson you wanted a transfer, because we talked about that. But I shouldn't have given you grief about it. I know why you did it."

"Love you."

My heart tripped, and I turned my hand over beneath hers and squeezed it. "I know. And I think I knew it then." I grimaced. "Maybe I did know, and was trying to pick a fight, without realizing I was doing it. It's convoluted, but it scared me that you would offer to do something like that for me, because I knew what that had to mean. It had nothing to do with the job, and everything to do with being so in love with someone again that you can't imagine life without them. When you love someone, it hurts when you lose them, and I've already lived through that once. But it's too late. You're in my heart already. Whether we're together or not, I'm always going to love you and I'm always going to worry about you." I waved my hand around all the machines. "Now more than ever. But not being with you is worse than worrying."

"Love me," she said, her words slurred as though she was going to drop off to sleep.

"I really do. You put my needs before yours, and it's what people in love do. I should've remembered, because I can think of a hundred times I did that for Seth and he did that for me. I would do the same for you."

"I . . . know." She blinked a few times and seemed to rally herself. "Ne . . . ver letting you go."

EPILOGUE

Four Months Later

I stepped in the door just past eleven, exhausted and starving. Work had been a madhouse the last few months, mostly because Eve was still on medical leave and, though I liked Delia, when it came to Community Relations, she was the fish out of water she readily admitted to being. A heavily pregnant and ready-to-pop-at-any-time fish who'd been placed on desk duty, so she'd been the logical person to step in while Eve healed, but because I was more familiar with it, most of the grunt work had fallen to me to handle, making the days long and tiring.

And since it was Monday, I'd had my class to teach at shul, which made for an even longer day.

Eve was in the family room, curled up on the sofa where we'd had our first tentative explorations together, asleep with her book against her chest. I watched her for a long moment, listened to her even breathing. Though she was nearly ready to go back to work—just waiting for medical clearance—there were days I still needed to reassure myself that she was alive. Today was one of those days, when I was exhausted and the worry in my mind took over.

I leaned down and kissed her cheek.

"Tal." She blinked awake and stretched, the book toppling to the floor. "I guess I fell asleep. What time is it?"

My anxiety eased, replaced with exhaustion. I yawned. "After eleven. I am *beat*." A long growl came from my stomach, and I grimaced. "And starving. I didn't expect to be this long, but when class was over I got roped into helping for a few hours at the homeless shelter until the regular volunteer got there. He had car trouble. Sorry I didn't call. My phone was dead."

She rose, gave me a quick hug and a kiss on my temple, then drew me to the kitchen and pushed me into a chair. Once I was seated, she grabbed a box from the fridge and slid it my way.

I lifted the lid and groaned in sheer ecstasy. Half a margherita pizza, which was just as good cold as hot. I practically inhaled the first slice, and Eve watched with a sleepy, amused look on her pillow-creased face.

She pushed away from the counter and grabbed a glass, then filled it with water and a splash of juice, exactly the way I liked it. "Drink it all, and I'll get you another. The pizza was good but salty."

"Thanks." I drained it and she filled it again. "I didn't get anything to drink, either. Nothing since about five."

"You need a keeper," Eve muttered, pinching the crust off one of the leftover slices.

"You volunteering?" I asked, sliding the box closer to me so she couldn't snitch any more. "Hands off my pizza."

"It was a peace offering because I know I've been cranky this last week, but if you're gonna be like that, I'm taking *my* pizza back," she said, swiping another piece of crust and hooking her finger over the box as though to draw it back to her side of the table. "And maybe."

"Fine. But the rest is mine." I relented, pushing the half-mangled slice to her. It took a moment and another bite of pizza for that *maybe* to click in my tired brain. *Maybe? What does* that *mean?*

We finished our pizza with a minimum of words, and then after she put the glass in the dishwasher and the box in the garbage, she took my hand. "Did you lock up?"

"Yes, ma'am."

"Good." She drew me down the hall to the bedroom, shucking her clothes until she was in nothing but panties and a cami, and slid into what was now her side of the bed with a groan. "I'm going to have heartburn from eating and laying right down, but I'm too damned tired to stay awake. And I know I should brush my teeth, but one night isn't going to kill me."

I gave a half-asleep grin, then changed my clothes for a big T-shirt. I used the toilet and climbed into bed beside her. "Brushing teeth takes too much energy, and I have about none." And since we both had garlic breath, I kissed her softly, and curled close to her, being extra careful not to bump her sometimes still-tender scars.

She cupped my face with her palm, then kissed me back. "I talked to the doctor today." She paused, swiped a thumb over my lips. "I'm cleared to go back to work next week if I'm up to it. Desk duty only, and then another checkup in two weeks."

My heart tripped. I knew she'd be going back to work someday, and she was ready . . . but I wasn't. The thought of her in the line of fire again about killed me. But I loved a cop, and that meant I had to deal with it. At least she'd be on limited duty for the first two weeks. "You think you'll be up to it?"

"God, yes. I'm going stir-crazy. I'm cleared to start running too. I'll start in PT tomorrow. Slow going, of course, but I'm crawling out of my skin with all this inactivity."

"I just need you to be careful. I don't think I'd survive losing you." I laced my fingers with hers and squeezed. "I love you, Eve."

"I love you too, Tal, and I'm not going anywhere. Go to sleep, and we'll figure out the rest tomorrow." She yawned, then flipped over onto her side, and we curled together like spoons, our legs entwined.

She fell asleep before I did, but I followed her about a minute or two later.

My alarm went off way too early, especially since we'd been up so late. I burrowed into the pillow and deeper under the covers, only to have the blanket yanked off me.

"Move it."

I groaned and pulled the pillow over my head. "You are *such* a tyrant."

Eve lifted the pillow and waved the mug in her hand under my nose. "You know you want this, addict."

Mmmmm, coffee. I grabbed blindly for it, but she held it out of my reach.

"Unh huh. You've got to get out of bed to get it."

I dropped my face back into the pillow. "If I'd known you were this cruel, I'd have looked for a different girlfriend."

The words came out somewhat mangled, but she must've gotten the gist because she laughed. "It'll be in the bathroom on the counter," she taunted, heading off to the bathroom.

I wanted to hurl the pillow at her, but that might spill my coffee. I glared at her, narrow-eyed. "Mean."

She laughed again, then tossed her panties and cami out the bathroom door at me. "Just wait 'til I start making you run with me. Move it, Wasserman."

I banged my head and groaned, then shoved my ass up and followed her to the bathroom. The steaming cup of coffee was right on the counter where she'd said it would be, next to a cup of hot tea. The devil in me considered pouring her tea down the toilet, but even I couldn't be that cruel.

So instead I turned on the hot water for about a second, sending a shot of cold into her shower. This old house had many things I loved about it, but the fact that the hot—or cold—water could only be one place at a time wasn't one of them.

She yelped, and I grinned and turned the hot water back off, sending her shower back to a normal temperature. I probably shouldn't have done it, considering she was still recovering, but her relieved groan made me laugh. And I fully expected she'd get me back for this. Maybe not today, because Eve was wily like that. She had the same devilish sense of humor I did, except that she was good at the long game, and I'd have already forgotten about the payback by the time she'd gotten her revenge.

Which meant I'd have to watch my back.

She stepped out of the shower and stalked close, not bothering with a towel.

"Eep," I said, backing up with a laugh. "Don't you dare."

She didn't listen and came forward, trapping me between her lusciously wet body and my robe hanging on the bathroom door. After lacing her fingers with mine and pressing our hands back against the door, she dipped her head, claiming my mouth in a fierce kiss that set my heart pounding and made my head go light.

She tasted of toothpaste and mint tea, and when she finally broke the kiss I took over, bending my head to lick the droplets of water from her neck and shoulder. We'd made love since she'd been released from the hospital, but always carefully, and this morning was no different. I sucked lightly on her collarbone, and she shuddered.

Her arms dropped as though her muscles had gone limp, and I took the opportunity to spin her so our positions were reversed, my mouth sucking on one stiffened nipple and then the other. I sucked lightly there too, and she rubbed her shower-wet thighs together. I smiled against her skin. "You let me know if anything hurts."

"I hurt," she said, brushing the back of her hand over her mound. "Right here."

I laughed, then dropped to my knees and buried my face between her legs, licking the water droplets from her thighs. I urged her to put a leg over my shoulder, which opened her even further to me. Then I licked right down her center, tonguing her until she came unglued, sagging against the door, her legs trembling.

"That . . . God." She put her foot back on the floor and I grabbed behind me for a towel. "What you do to me."

She went to take it but I held it out of her reach, staying on my knees as I dried her off, working from her feet up to her torso, kissing the same path the towel did, being especially careful around the puckered scars on her chest and her arm, the scars that always made me realize just how close I'd come to losing her. When she locked eyes with me, the heat in them was nearly my undoing. I wanted her again, and someday soon we'd get back to the mattress marathons we'd had before she got hurt, but I could tell that one round had tired her out. And besides, one round was all we had time for. "Don't give me that face. I'm late already."

She ran a finger along my cheek. "Officially, you don't start until eight. I know you're usually there early, but . . . "

She was right, but I shook my head. "I have a school visit today, remember. But later tonight? I'm all yours." I stood, then finished toweling her off, paying extra special attention around her breasts.

Her breathing hitched, and she laugh-moaned and grabbed the towel from me. "Tal. You're not helping."

"Tell me about it," I muttered. "I gotta shower before I change my mind."

She laughed again and kissed me hard, shoving me toward the shower.

I took a quick one, then hurriedly dried myself and dressed in khaki pants and my Community Relations T-shirt, which was no longer as tight as it had been when Eve had given it to me. I'd lost about fifteen pounds after the shooting and during Eve's recovery. I didn't mind the lost weight, but I hoped never to be in that situation again.

When I got to the kitchen, Eve had breakfast ready on the counter.

I frowned. "I should be taking care of you, not the other way around."

"It's a bagel and an orange. Pretty sure I can manage that." She rolled her eyes and sighed. "I wish I was going with you."

"I know." I kissed her cheek and snagged a bagel half slathered with veggie cream cheese, exactly how I liked it. "Soon."

She leaned against the counter next to me, nibbling on the granola cereal she liked. "Derrick called last night."

"He did? What's up?" I'd spent a lot of time with him while Eve was in the hospital. When he'd first gone back overseas, I'd talked with him daily, keeping him updated on Eve's progress. Now that she was better, we texted and talked often, sometimes about her, sometimes about Gabriela and their wedding plans, and sometimes about nothing in particular. He was the son I'd never had, and I loved him very much.

"He said Lila sent him and Gabriela another care package. One of the guys in his unit loves her cookies and wants to meet her." She grinned, paused, and studied me. "He also wanted to know if I was going to sell my duplex."

I stilled. While she'd stayed with me after she'd been released from the hospital, once she'd started driving again, she'd also been spending time at her own place, claiming she needed some space. I understood it, but I wanted her to move in with me, fully. I hated being apart from her. "What did you say?"

She looked at me over her tea, then flashed me that devilish grin I loved so much. "I told him I was waiting for my girlfriend to make an honest woman out of me, and once that happened, then I'd make a decision." She dropped a square box on the counter, pushed it toward me. "I'm tired of waiting. Open it."

I blinked, and opened it. Inside the box were two identical necklaces, each with intertwined hearts, one gold, one silver. My heart thudded and my eyes swam. "Oh, Eve."

Her eyes were suspiciously bright too. "I love you, Talia Wasserman. I know I should've waited and done this right, but I want to be with you the rest of my life. We'll figure out the house thing but I don't want to wait anymore. Marry me?"

I lost the fight and a few tears fell over, but they were happy tears. Never, ever had I imagined I'd be this lucky twice in a lifetime. "Yes, yes, yes." I hugged her tight, kissed her, then leaned my forehead against hers. "I love you, Eve Poe, my badass cop. And we can live wherever you want. Here, your place, or somewhere new. I don't care, as long as we're together."

She picked up one of the necklaces and put it around my neck, and I did the same for her. We grinned at each other like fools, and then we kissed again.

"So I was thinking maybe we should get married when Derrick and Gabri do," Eve said.

I smacked her uninjured arm.

She rubbed it, glaring at me. "Ow. What was that for?"

I rolled my eyes. "You are not doing that to our future daughter-in-law. She and Derrick deserve their own day."

"Mean." Her eyes glinted with mirth, and she bumped my hip. "I didn't want to wait that long anyway. We'll work that out later. Because one of us has to go to work, and it's not me."

I smirked. "Bossy thing."

She kissed the tip of my nose, then brushed her lips against mine. "And don't you forget it."

"Never," I vowed. "I love you."

"Love you too."

Dear Reader,

Thank you for reading Jodie Griffin's *Twice in a Lifetime*!

We know your time is precious and you have many, many entertainment options, so it means a lot that you've chosen to spend your time reading. We really hope you enjoyed it.

We'd be honored if you'd consider posting a review—good or bad—on sites like **Amazon, Barnes & Noble, Kobo, Goodreads, Twitter, Facebook, Tumblr,** and your blog or website. We'd also be honored if you told your friends and family about this book. Word of mouth is a book's lifeblood!

For more information on upcoming releases, author interviews, blog tours, contests, giveaways, and more, please sign up for our weekly, spam-free newsletter and visit us around the web:

Newsletter: tinyurl.com/RiptideSignup
Twitter: twitter.com/RiptideBooks
Facebook: facebook.com/RiptidePublishing
Goodreads: tinyurl.com/RiptideOnGoodreads
Tumblr: riptidepublishing.tumblr.com

Thank you so much for Reading the Rainbow!

RiptidePublishing.com

ACKNOWLEDGMENTS

I might've come up with the idea for this story, but to get a book written takes a cast of more than one.

I couldn't have gotten this one written without Tamsen, Sasha, Joy, Ericka, Michele, Jennifer and Cathy. They helped me turn Talia and Eve into real people with a real story to share.

And I couldn't have spent the time I needed to on it without my family's understanding that I needed them to go OUT so I could stay IN to write/edit.

Sarah Lyons was incredibly patient and understanding when my mother passed away in the middle of the submission/developmental edits process, and Carole-ann Galloway and the entire Riptide team have been amazing and I'm honored to be able to work with them.

My super-agent Courtney Miller-Callihan held my hand and answered about eleventy-billion questions on contracts and royalties and timelines.

My sincere thanks to all of you.

Also by JODIE GRIFFIN

Forbidden Fantasies
Forbidden Desires
Forbidden Fires
Forbidden Obsessions
Matzoh and Mistletoe

About THE AUTHOR

Jodie Griffin didn't always want to be a writer. She spent hours reading, but school papers were written one painful word at a time. Then a story idea came, demanding to be put on paper. After years of practice, she took the leap, submitted her first manuscript and hasn't looked back.

Jodie is also an avid photographer, a chocoholic, and a lover of bad puns. When she's not writing, she's likely out stalking the moon for that perfect shot.

Jodie's own happily-ever-after includes one incredibly supportive husband and one future heroine. Visit Jodie at jodiegriffin.com.

Facebook: facebook.com/Jodie-Griffin-165472856805202
Twitter: twitter.com/Jodie_Griffin
Tumblr: jodiegriffin.tumblr.com
Pinterest: pinterest.com/jodiegriffin
Instagram: instagram.com/authorjodiegriffin

Enjoy more stories like
Twice in a Lifetime
at RiptidePublishing.com!

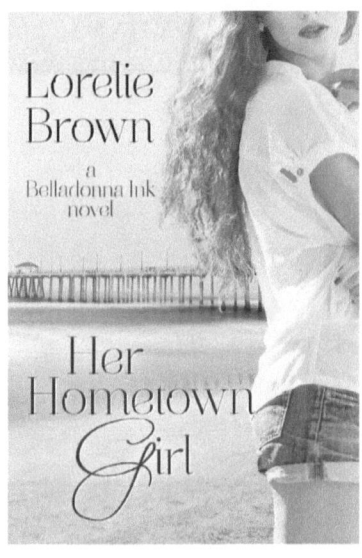

Her Hometown Girl
ISBN: 978-1-62649-647-7

Heat Wave
ISBN: 978-1-62649-516-6

Earn Bonus Bucks!

Earn 1 Bonus Buck for each dollar you spend. Find out how at RiptidePublishing.com/news/bonus-bucks.

Win Free Ebooks for a Year!

Pre-order coming soon titles directly through our site and you'll receive one entry into a drawing for a chance to win free books for a year! Get the details at RiptidePublishing.com/contests.